PUFFIN BOOKS

Magic with Everything

Cat is the sort of nanny any child would love to have. But, as Jess points out, 'She won't obey the rules!', which sometimes leads to trouble. (Like the time she leaves the green man at a pedestrian crossing curled up in the corner of his frame, the sign reading SLEEP NOW, while a lullaby plays.)

When Catriona first breezes into their lives, Jess, Toby and Flora don't know what's hit them. Suddenly there are plenty of good things to eat, new friends to enjoy, and lots of exciting things to do. Life is so much more relaxed, more fun, under Cat's tender, if often rather scatty, care and for once the children are allowed to be themselves.

But where did she come from? And where did she learn such an extraordinary brand of magic?

MAGIC
with
EVERYTHING

Roger Burt

PUFFIN BOOKS

*This book is for the girls of the real St Cat's –
St Catherine's School, Camberley, some of
whom are rather like Jess and some of whom
are likely to grow up to be rather like Cat.*

PUFFIN BOOKS

Published by the Penguin Group
Penguin Books Ltd, 27 Wrights Lane, London W8 5TZ, England
Penguin Putnam Inc., 375 Hudson Street, New York, New York 10014, USA
Penguin Books Australia Ltd, Ringwood, Victoria, Australia
Penguin Books Canada Ltd, 10 Alcorn Avenue, Toronto, Ontario, Canada M4V 3B2
Penguin Books (NZ) Ltd, Cnr Rosedale and Airborne Roads, Albany,
Auckland, New Zealand

Penguin Books Ltd, Registered Offices: Harmondsworth, Middlesex, England

First published by Blackie and Son Ltd 1990
Published in Puffin Books 1992
Reissued in Puffin Books 1998
1 3 5 7 9 10 8 6 4 2

Puffin Film and TV Tie-in edition first published 1998

Made and printed in England by Clays Ltd, St Ives plc

British Library Cataloguing in Publication Data
A CIP catalogue record for this book is available from the British Library

ISBN 0–141–30295–X

Contents

1

The First Day

'I am Catriona,' said the beautiful young woman, 'and I am your fairy godmother. You may call me Cat. Things are going to be different around here from now on.'

Toby and Jess looked at one another with foreboding. Flora sucked her thumb.

'Another nutter!' whispered Toby.

'At least she's prettier than the last one,' hissed Jess from behind her hand.

The last one had been Miss Grubb, tall, thin, elderly and mad. She had drunk all of Uncle Oz's secret supply of whisky and he had sacked her.

'You're not really a fairy godmother,' said Toby.

'Why not?' said Cat, chin in the air and green eyes flashing.

'Well, nobody is. There's no such thing. And anyway, you don't look like a fairy!'

'So *you* say,' sniffed Cat. 'What do fairies look like, according to you?'

'There aren't any – I told you.'

Jess said, 'I had a book once, when I was little, fairy stories and things like that, you know, and it had pictures in it of fairies . . . They were like – well, you know – like little girls in floaty dresses, with wings . . .' Her voice trailed off as she caught Cat's look of scorn.

'Oh, *those*!' said Cat, curling her lip. 'Soppy things. I am nothing like that whatever, I can assure you. I am a fairy godmother of the old school, I am, and when I say jump, you jump.'

'She doesn't look old to me,' whispered Jess. 'She's quite young. About twenty, I should think.'

'I don't believe any of it,' said Toby stubbornly. 'She's off her rocker.'

'You'd better believe it, kiddo,' said Cat. 'I have been sent to save you.'

'Save us? How do you mean?' said Jess doubtfully.

'You'll see. All will become clear in the due passage of time, my little primrose. You have been in grave danger of being bored to death, I hear. We shall have to change all that. Now, please help me to move in.'

They all trooped down into the street.

'This is Mini,' announced Cat, indicating a little grey car, much streaked with rust, that crouched on the double yellow lines at the kerb. 'She is very old, and you must treat her with the respect due to her wisdom and experience.'

Toby rolled his eyes skyward. 'Potty!' he muttered. 'Told you!'

Gradually, Cat's belongings were transferred from the little car to the room in the attic which was reserved for the Nanny. Jess and Toby panted up the flights of steep, narrow stairs with a succession of cardboard boxes carelessly tied up with loose string, untidy parcels, and tatty plastic carrier bags.

'Whatever is all this stuff?' said Toby, when they were up in the attic and Cat was safely down, rootling in Mini's boot.

'Clothes, mostly, I think,' said Jess, 'and make-up.

She's got some smashing things. And there seems to be a lot of biscuits and fruit and drinks and stuff.'

Cat appeared with the last box. 'I would like an hour or so to arrange my room, so take this box of food away and eat it, or the peaches and bananas will go bad. The chocolate biscuits are already melting. Such hot weather, isn't it?'

Flora pulled her thumb out of her mouth with a plop, and her eyes grew round. Chocolate biscuits!

'We're not allowed to eat between meals,' said Jess hesitantly, her mouth watering at the thought of peaches. 'Thank you very much all the same.'

'Who says?' asked Cat, quite sharply.

'Well – Aunt Spot – er, that is, Aunt Matilda. She says it's bad for our teeth and Toby is too fat.'

'I'm *not*!' hissed Toby furiously. 'I am not fat! I'm *stocky*. I'm well-built. And you're a skinny Lizzie with legs like celery.'

'Look, I'm in charge now,' said Cat firmly, 'and what I say goes. Eat the food. Throw the skins and bits away so no one will know. Just remember – I'm the boss, and *I* can do *anything*.'

'Oh yeah?' said Toby to Jess, on the way down to the day-room. 'I bet she won't do anything with Aunt Spot. I bet what she says won't go with *her*.'

Cat rejoined the children in the day-room just before tea, looking cool, fresh and very pretty in a light summer frock.

'Excuse me,' said Jess timidly, 'don't you wear a uniform? Nanny Grubb did.'

'I am not a Nanny,' said Cat firmly. 'Nor a governess nor a nurse nor a teacher. I am not an au-pair girl or a child-minder. I've told you, I'm your fairy godmother. Well – sort of fairy. And sort of godmother. You'll see. And I wear what I jolly well like.'

'What sort of fairy?' Toby wanted to know.

'My sort,' said Cat. 'And that's the end of it, unless you want to be a frog.'

Toby opened his mouth to reply, and then shut it again. Cat smiled, with slitted eyes. 'I wonder what's for tea?' she said.

Cross-eyed Mrs Dooley came puffing and panting up the stairs with the children's tea on a tray, which she banged down on the table; she staggered away again, eyes more crossed than ever and blowing hard. 'These here stairs'll be the death of me,' they heard her moan as she began her laborious descent. She always said that, always on the third stair down.

'And what, exactly,' said Cat, poking things on the tray, 'is this?'

'Our tea,' said Toby miserably.

'Bread and marge and rock buns,' said Jess.

'They're Mrs Dooley Specials, those buns,' said Toby. 'You can't eat 'em. We generally chuck 'em out of the window at next door's dog. *He* can't eat 'em, either,' he added bitterly.

'It's the same every day,' warned Jess.

'Salty porridge for breakfast,' said Toby.

'Mince for lunch,' went on Jess, 'with watery potatoes and soggy cabbage.'

'Followed by semolina pudding,' said Toby, pulling awful faces. 'Every day! Slippery slobbery semolina! Snoddy-gobbles! Blegh!'

'And this is tea!' wailed Jess, pointing.

'We get so hungry,' said Toby, fiercely.

'And Flora cries when she smells cabbage,' said Jess in tones of deep despair.

Cat said nothing for a moment, and then, 'This is just what we need. We'll go and feed the ducks. Come on.'

The thick slabs of bread-and-margarine and the inedible rock buns disappeared into Cat's shiny plastic carrier-bag. She stood up. 'Well? What are you waiting for? We'll have tea on the way, never fear. Where's Flora's pushchair?'

That was the first time they went to Mario's. They would never forget the first time, especially Jess, because she was absolutely overcome with shyness to begin with. Mario's was so posh that it had menus with no prices on them; only very rich people could afford it. Jess would never have dared to go in there, never in a million years. Cat didn't care, though. She breezed in as if she owned the place, sweeping the children along with her, pushchair and all, and sat them all down at a table, bang in the middle of the room. Everyone stared at them and Jess went red.

Cat smiled at the waiters and beckoned. At once, three of them rushed over, practically fighting each other to be the first to serve Cat. She smiled a lot more and her eyes sparkled – she obviously adored all the attention. She turned to the handsomest waiter.

'Pancakes, first,' she ordered, 'and plenty of 'em. Then cream cakes and puddings and trifle and all that.'

The handsome waiter bowed and spoke in Italian to the other two, and – before the children had had time to recover their breath – a trolley was brought to the table, bearing a little spirit-burner and a copper frying-pan and all the things needed to cook the pancakes before their very eyes. The waiter, whose name was Toni, as Cat very soon found out, poured brandy on each pancake as it was cooked and set fire to it. Flora squealed with glee and clapped, every time.

'You like Toni's pancakes?' he said, bowing low to Flora and smiling widely.

'Lovely lovely lovely!' shouted Flora at the top of her voice, stopping all conversation at the other tables.

'Good! Excellent! Mister Mario will be pleased with Toni! Some more?'

The pancakes were out of this world. They ate dozens. They ate them until they thought they would burst, and pleased Toni no end (he was especially pleased with Toby). When another trolley was wheeled in, this time laden with fruit and cakes and chocolate things, everyone was too full to try more than a few. Except Toby.

'Can we come here again?' he asked, polishing his bowl with his spoon.

'You bet,' said Cat. 'Every day. Won't catch *me* eating Dooley Specials.'

Toni came with the bill on a little silver dish. Cat paid with a credit card.

'Isn't it clever?' she said. 'You don't have to have any money – the little plastic card will do just as well. I do find the twentieth century so convenient.'

They *thought* she was joking.

Later, at bedtime, Toby said to Jess, 'She must be completely barmy, going on about being a fairy an' all, but I reckon she's going to be fun. She certainly knows how to eat, for one thing. I just wonder what else she can do?'

2

Cat Takes Charge

Aunt Spot wasn't really their Aunt and Spot wasn't her name. They called her that because they hated her and she had a pimple on her chin, round, pink and sharply pointed. Sometimes it grew larger, and then dwindled again.

'Like the phases of the moon,' said Toby, 'or the Great Red Spot on Jupiter.'

She always called Toby 'Tobias' and Jess 'Jessica', which they hated too, so they got their own back by calling her Aunt Spot whenever she wasn't there to hear them. Her name was actually Miss Matilda Murgatroyd; she was Uncle Oz's sister and had never married. Uncle Oz wasn't their real Uncle, either, and he was unmarried, too, which should be no surprise to anybody because he was really horrible. They were the only relations the lawyers could find to take care of the children after their parents had been killed.

It was surprising that they had agreed to look after the children at all, since they both loathed anyone younger than about sixty; but money had a lot to do with it. There was quite a small fortune, as it turned out, because the children's parents had been well insured when the plane crash happened. Most of it was being kept by the lawyers for when the children grew up. However, Uncle Oz and Aunt Spot had been given enough to provide a 'good home' for them – that is, dusty old Number 13 – and to pay the fees at rotten, boring, stinking St Stithian's School; and the lawyers paid an allowance to cover the costs of their clothes and food, which Aunt Spot cheated over like mad.

'Aunt Spot is a sad case,' said Cat after she'd been with them for a few days. 'She needs doing good to.'

'Why?' said Toby, scandalised. 'She's a mean old drivelling old ratbag. She never does good to *us*.'

'Exactly,' said Cat. 'She's fairly asking for it.' And she bundled them all out of the house and round to the television shop.

'I'm blowed if I know how her mind works,' whispered Jess. 'What on earth are we doing *here*, of all places?'

Aunt Spot was dead set against television, of course; after all, it might give pleasure. 'The growing mind requires nourishment, Tobias. Flickering images are no substitute for *work*, Jessica. And little Florinda must grow up in purity and goodness, away from corrupting influences.'

If you mentioned television to Uncle Oz, he just jingled his change and muttered, 'Carnaffordit,' into his moustache.

'They'll be putting up the aerials tomorrow morning, and the sets will arrive straight after that,' announced Cat as they left the shop. '*Such* a nice man – so helpful.'

Toby gazed up at her with his mouth open; Jess exclaimed, 'But Aunt Spot'll go mad!' Flora just gurgled.

'No, she won't,' said Cat confidently. '*I've* paid for it all, with my little credit card.'

'You know,' said Toby quietly to Jess, 'I don't think she understands about credit cards. Not how they work, I mean. She's spending money like water.'

Jess said, 'She just doesn't *care*. Oh, I do hope it's all right – we won't get into trouble, will we? They won't send us to prison?'

The aerials were fixed up early the next morning.

Cat was delighted, and made a great fuss of the workman. 'Can you ask the shop to send the sets round right away?' she said, fluttering her eyelashes. She smiled, and Jess could see her little pointed teeth.

'For you, darlin' – anything!' said the man, and winked. Jess thought he was rather rude, but Cat liked it.

'Isn't it dreadful,' whispered Jess, 'the way she makes eyes at all the men.' But Toby didn't understand what she was talking about.

Very soon, the sets arrived. There was an enormous one in a wooden cabinet for Aunt Spot, on its own trolley, and several of different sizes which disappeared into Cat's attic. The children had one each, pretty little white portables, so that they wouldn't quarrel about which channel to have on.

'They're all colour sets, of course,' said Cat casually. 'I do think the twentieth century is wonderful. *Such* a nice man, wasn't he?'

Toby and Jess confidently expected Aunt Spot to explode, like an atom bomb, devastating whole areas of the city, but she didn't; Cat had arranged for the huge set to be plugged in and working when Aunt Spot first set eyes on it, and she was captivated from the start.

'She gibbered a bit to begin with,' said Jess, 'but

Cat just turned up the volume so that she couldn't be heard, and within seconds she was sitting absolutely riveted to some awful drivel about flower-arranging.'

'She loves it,' Cat reported. 'I knew she would. It's nice and loud, so she can hear every word – and she can't hear *us*, which is a good thing.'

It was true. With Aunt Spot glued to her thundering telly all day and half the night they could run up and down stairs and shout and fight and be thoroughly normal and naughty.

They very quickly found out that, although watching television was entertaining, watching Aunt Spot watch television was even more fun.

'She thinks it's real!' said Toby, rolling his eyes upward. 'She talks back at it! She's going off her trolley, you know. She thinks there are real little people in there! I've tried telling her all about it, about radio waves and aerials and that, but she won't listen. She gets cross and says "Hush, Tobias, the gentleman is speaking, Tobias. Do not interrupt your elders. Children should be seen and not heard, Tobias." Daft old bat.'

Aunt Spot's life was changed by television. She fell hopelessly in love with two news-readers and all of the weathermen. It did her good.

'Good evening,' the news-reader would say.

'Good *evening*,' Aunt Spot would reply, coyly.

'Here is the news,' the man would continue.

'Oh, how kind! Thank you *so* much!' Aunt Spot would sigh, her heart going pit-a-pat.

'I told you!' yelled Cat down the stairs one night when the children should have been in bed but weren't. 'I *told* you it would do her good!'

'Ooh, that Cat!' exclaimed Jess. 'She's wicked!'

*

'I must go to the library today,' said Jess one morning. 'My book will be overdue tomorrow.' She was terrified of library fines, partly because Aunt Spot never gave her any pocket money, and Jess thought that if she couldn't pay they would send her to prison.

'Oh – what fun!' exclaimed Cat. 'Let's go at once. We didn't have libraries on Muckle Eigg – at least, not like yours.'

'What's Mucky Egg?' enquired Toby.

'It's where I come from,' said Cat absent-mindedly, poking about in a cupboard. 'Have you seen my carrier bag? It's got some Dooley Specials in it, for the ducks.'

As they left the house, Toby asked, 'Are we going in your car?' Mini crouched in the gutter amid the rubbish, shedding rust.

'Oh, take no notice of her,' said Cat dismissively. 'She's sulking. Won't start, and says she doesn't want to go anywhere, ever again. She'll be all right in a bit. Her sulks generally last about three days.'

Toby, behind Cat's back, rolled his eyes heavenwards and tapped the side of his head. Jess giggled, but she thought Mini did look a bit down-in-the-mouth; her little radiator grill looked plain grumpy.

'Come on,' said Cat, giving Flora's pushchair a healthy shove. 'It's a beautiful day, and I feel frisky.'

'Why is she so excited about the library, for heaven's sake?' whispered Toby, as they stood in the High Street waiting for the lights to change. 'She must have seen a library before. I mean, *everybody's* seen a *library*.'

He was interrupted by a delighted squeal from Cat.

17

'Oh – look! Look at the little green man! Isn't that just fantastic!'

The WALK NOW sign flashed on and went beep-beep-beep, but Cat still stood there enchanted as people swirled all around her and rushed across.

The lights changed.

'He's gone! What a shame. Will he come back?'

Toby goggled. 'Of course he will. You just have to press the button and wait. Don't you know *that*? It usually takes a long time. Don't you have these crossings where you come from?'

'Frogface, we don't even have *roads* on Muckle Eigg. Here, let's speed this thing up.'

'I told you, it usually takes a long—' Toby began, but Cat, frowning, was doing something to the metal box which controlled the lights. She seemed to be poking about inside it with a thin knitting needle.

'Hey! What are you up to?' exclaimed Toby, glasses flashing.

'Oh, Cat – you mustn't,' said Jess anxiously. 'You'll get into trouble.'

'Shut up – I'm concentrating,' said Cat, showing the tip of her pointy pink tongue as she poked away. 'I think I'm just getting the hang of this . . .'

Suddenly, the air was filled with the squealing of brakes and the blaring of horns, as the traffic snarled to a halt.

'There!' said Cat triumphantly. 'Now – let's see what the little green man can do.'

She pushed the button and watched the WALK NOW sign eagerly. It flickered, went blank, and then said RUN NOW. The little green man ran frantically. Another push. HOP NOW, ordered the sign; he hopped. Cat began to laugh aloud with pleasure. Jess caught her arm.

The honking of horns grew furious; taxi drivers and bus conductors were yelling; people in the crowd were laughing and pointing. The beep-beep mechanism began to play band music. MARCH NOW said the sign; the little green man turned upside down and marched on his hands. A policeman drew near, scowling under his helmet.

'Grab her, Toby,' yelled Jess, but Toby was quite helpless with laughter. Jess tugged furiously at Cat's arm and somehow managed to pull her with one hand and the pushchair with the other across the road to the safety of the park on the other side.

Toby's laughter turned into hiccups.

'You are a spoilsport, Jess,' Cat complained. 'I was really enjoying that. I'm sure I could have had him talking in a jiffy. Whistling, at any rate.'

'We shall have to keep an eye on her,' Jess muttered to Toby. 'She just isn't responsible!'

'Hic,' said Toby.

Cat was fascinated by the computer system at the library. Toby explained:

'You get a little pink card. When you take a book out, the computer reads your card, and it reads the magnetic strip on the book through a sort of pen thing, so it knows who's got which book. And when you bring your book back it reads it all again and then it knows you've returned it. Simple.'

'You are clever, Toby,' said Cat admiringly. 'Fancy knowing all that. Isn't he clever, Jess? How many can you take out at once?'

'Three, I think,' said Toby.

'And how long for?'

'Two weeks.'

Cat was thoughtful. 'That's no use,' she muttered. 'We shall have to alter that.'

While Jess and Toby browsed, and Flora happily chewed a rag book in the Tinies Section, Cat strolled over to the main reception desk and leaned casually against it.

'She's up to something,' said Jess, sounding worried. 'I do wish she wouldn't. And she's flirting with the library man.'

When they left, Cat's bag and Flora's pushchair were stuffed with books.

'Look,' Cat said, proudly showing them a pink library card. 'This is mine! Isn't it pretty? Such a delicate colour.'

'How many books have you got?' said Toby suspiciously.

'Oh, about thirty. Or forty. I didn't count.'

'But you *can't*,' said Jess. 'You're only allowed three!'

'Not me,' said Cat with a self-satisfied smile. 'I had a little word with the computer. We understand one another. Wasn't the librarian handsome? Such a nice man!'

'They'll all have to go back in a fortnight, you know,' warned Toby.

'Not so, my little pudding. They're all stamped for three years,' Cat said nonchalantly over her shoulder. 'Come along, Flora-dora – duck-stuffing time!'

'Breeee!' said Flora, piercingly.

'She's *impossible*,' said Jess, shaking her head. 'She won't obey *rules*.'

After feeding the ducks Cat wanted to play with

the pedestrian crossing again, but Jess wouldn't let her. The sign read SLEEP NOW and the little green man was curled up in the corner of his frame. The beep-beep mechanism played a gentle lullaby. The policeman, perspiring freely, stood with his helmet pushed back, scratching his head amid the snarled-up traffic.

'Oh, Cat – just look what you've done!' wailed Jess.

Toby got the hiccups again.

'It does people good, you know, to have a little excitement,' was all Cat would say.

3

The People Collection

'What are you going to do about Mrs Dooley?'

'Shut up, Toby!' hissed Jess, kicking him under the table. They were having tea at Mario's again.

'I think she needs doing good to,' said Cat with her mouth full.

'What do you mean?' said Jess anxiously.

Cat was just going to explain when Mario himself came to their table and began a long, whispered conversation, with much bowing and scraping, terribly polite although he did look awfully determined about something. Cat developed a slight frown. 'Oh, dear,' they heard her say, and, 'How much?' and, 'Oh, I am sorry!' and, 'Don't worry – tomorrow at the latest.'

'It's to do with my little credit card,' she told them when Mario had gone away again. 'I don't really understand it, but Mario seems to think it isn't any good any more. Perhaps it's broken. Anyway, we could do with a nice lot of money. I think I know where we can get some.'

'Where?' said Jess in tones of the direst foreboding.

'Where?' said Toby excitedly, glasses flashing with glee.

'I'll show you. Off we go – it isn't far. I've seen people getting it out of a hole in the wall.'

*

The 'hole in the wall' was the cash dispenser outside one of the big banks in the High Street.

'You can't use that,' said Toby flatly.

'Course I can. I can do anything.'

'No you can't. You have to have a special card and a computer code and I don't know what-all.'

'I've got this card, haven't I? Such a pretty pink. It'll do.'

Toby stood with his arms folded and a superior smirk on his face. Cat inserted her library card and slipped her hand somewhere inside the cash dispenser. The knitting needle flashed. Jess looked sick.

Cat frowned, and closed her eyes. 'Gosh, isn't it complicated,' she murmured. The machine beeped and chirruped, and there were whirring noises. Cat said, 'Ah – got it! That should do the trick. It should be coming . . . *now*!'

She held out her plastic carrier bag as bundles and bundles of brand-new notes cascaded all over the place. They filled the bag, and rained down over the pushchair, and bounced off Flora onto the pavement.

'That'll do,' said Cat, thumping the cash dispenser. 'Come on, you kids. Help me to fill the pushchair.'

Toby and Jess walked a long way behind Cat and Flora on the way home, in case the Flying Squad appeared. Jess was close to tears with anxiety. 'She'll get caught, I know she will, and she'll get sent to prison, and we'll get into dreadful trouble, and Aunt Spot and Uncle Oz'll kick us out, and then what will become of us all?'

Toby said nothing. He was too stunned by the sight of so much money.

Jess said. 'She's got no morals, that's her trouble. She's wicked!'

*

In the morning, Jess and Toby found Cat in the kitchen with, of all people, Toni. They hardly knew which questions to ask first.

'Why are you up so early?'

'What's Toni doing here?'

'Where's Mrs Dooley?'

'Have the police come round yet?'

'What's happened to all that money?'

'I am up early,' said Cat indistinctly, licking her spoon, 'to teach Toni how to make decent porridge. It should be served with cream and sugar – or possibly golden syrup – not too hot and not too cold, but just right. Baby Bear had all his marbles, I can tell you. Toni's awfully good at it already – you must try some. Mrs Dooley has gone. She said to Aunt Spot, "I'm going to retire, Mum, and live with me sister in Blackpool. I can't abide them stairs no more, Mum. It's me legs, see."'

Cat stopped imitating Mrs Dooley to giggle. 'I'll have some more, please, Toni – it's absolutely delish. I took her in to see Aunt Spot last night just before News At Ten. Aunt Spot was *furious*, because she's in love with the announcer, so she would have agreed to anything, just to get rid of us. "Whatever you want, my good woman," she said to Mrs Dooley. "Pray do not let me detain you!" We were out of there in twenty seconds flat.'

'But the *money*!' pleaded Jess. 'The *police*!'

'What police? The money's all gone. Mrs Dooley had most of it, naturally.'

'Why?' demanded Toby, horrified. It seemed utterly insane to give it to her.

'For her retirement, of course. She wouldn't have gone, otherwise – couldn't afford to.'

'Oh! I see,' said Toby.

'But that's bribery!' gasped Jess. 'Isn't that against the law?'

'Rot! It'll do her good . . . And it'll certainly do us good. It's going to do Toni good, too, isn't that right?'

'Sure thing!' said Toni, grinning so that his white teeth flashed.

'Toni has always wanted to be a chef, you see, not just a waiter, even at Mario's. Mario had a lot of money too, because of my credit card being broken and I gave him some more because he was sorry Toni was leaving, and I gave Toni a lot of pay in advance and quite a lot more for the shopping . . . I think that's all. Oh – and there was the fifty quid Flora chewed up on the way home last night.'

There didn't seem to be much that anyone could say; and Toni's porridge was very, very good – even Flora ate two bowlfuls.

Cat smiled. 'That was really delicious.' She stretched. 'Beautiful day again . . . Let's take Flora for a walk and leave Toni in peace to make the lunch. You can show me some more exciting twentieth-century things – I *loved* the library.'

'Hm!' said Jess. 'All right. But only if you promise to behave yourself.'

'Oh, I will, I will!' said Cat innocently. But she smiled, showing teeth.

On the way to the shops Toby and Cat would have liked to stop to watch the workmen who were trying to repair the little green man, but Jess dragged them off. The sign said CAKE NOW and the little green man appeared to be eating. It looked like fun. However, Jess was still in a highly nervous state.

Flora shouted, 'Puppy dogs! Wanna see puppy dogs!'

'They're in a pet-shop window,' explained Jess. 'Come on, Cat – come *away* from there!'

'Spoilsport,' said Cat.

'Really!' Jess whispered to Toby. '*We* have to look after *her*. It's *supposed* to be the other way *round*!'

In her agitation, Jess had forgotten that they would have to pass the bank on the way to the pet-shop.

'Oh, super!' said Cat. 'We can get some more money.'

'Absolutely not!' yelled Jess. Even Toby agreed.

'You mustn't, you know, Cat,' he said. 'It's stealing. You'll get into awful trouble.'

'It's a criminal *offence*!' said Jess desperately. 'It's daylight *robbery*! We'll all get sent to *prison*!'

'Oh, phooey! I don't see any harm in it. The computer doesn't mind. We got on famously together, didn't you notice?'

'But it doesn't *belong* to the computer!'

'Who does it belong to, then? You?'

'Don't be silly – it belongs to the bank,' shouted Toby, red in the face with the effort of trying to make Cat understand. 'You're not *allowed* to steal from banks – it's a terrible *crime*!'

'I don't see why. It doesn't do any harm – in fact, it does a lot of good. I like doing good. Look – we've done good to Mrs Dooley, and Toni's happy, and Mario's happy, and *we're* all happy, and the computer's delighted. All that happiness, and you say it's wrong! I don't understand kids. It's a good thing I got all those books from the library.'

'What books?'

'The Child Psychology ones.'

'Good grief!' was all that Toby could say.

By then they had arrived at the bank. Jess was relieved to see that the cash dispenser had a big OUT OF ORDER sign on the wall above it, and white-coated men had its front panel off and appeared to be testing the machinery inside.

'Oh, dear,' said Cat. 'There must be something wrong with it.'

'I'll say there is,' muttered Toby under his breath. 'It dishes out thousands of quid to mad women with knitting needles, that's what's wrong with it . . .'

In charge was a tall, slim man in a smart suit. He had a lapel badge which read 'Mr J. Menon'.

'What a smashing man!' breathed Cat. 'I *must* talk to him. He looks just like Omar Sharif.'

'Who's he?' said Toby.

'Come *away*!' squeaked Jess. Mr Menon had dark, intelligent eyes, and looked very sharp indeed. He would see through Cat, she was sure. There would be trouble . . .

'Go and look at the puppy dogs with Flora, you two. I just know that Mr Menon and I have lots in common and lots to talk about. See you at lunch-time.'

'Well!' said Jess. 'Abandoned. Just like that. That Cat has no scruples.'

'I've bought a computer,' announced Cat when they were back in the kitchen, eating Toni's prawns-cooked-in-batter. 'Only a little one for starters. It's up in my room.'

'What did you use for money?' enquired Jess suspiciously.

'Lib'ry card,' said Cat through prawns.

'What do you want a computer for?' said Toby.

'To do good with.'

'How?'

'Dunno, yet. They're nice and complicated, though. There's so much scope with complicated things – so much they can *do*. Bound to be good.'

'Like you did with the little green man, I suppose?' said Jess sarcastically. 'He was going backwards when we came home and the sign said WON KLAW.'

'Exactly. That made a lot of people happy and it provided useful employment for the repair men. It did a lot of good. These prawns are delicious – got any more?'

'Well, how are you going to do good with a micro-computer?'

'I'm not absolutely sure, yet, but that charming Mr Menon is going to come round and teach me how to use it. He's a computer expert, you know – frightfully clever. Such a nice man.'

So that was how Mr Menon got himself collected. He spent many hours with Cat, in his spare time, trying to explain about micro-chips, printed circuits and all the rest of it. Cat soon realised that her first machine was too small for her requirements, whatever they were.

'Well, it only has a 48K memory,' she said with a superior sniff. 'Kids' stuff!'

Mr Menon brought bits of this and that with him every time he came round, and Cat went on buying sprees until her attic was overflowing with electronics.

'How are you paying for all this?' Jess inquired, with narrowed eyes. 'You're not robbing banks on the quiet, are you?'

'Oh, no – I use my credit card. It wasn't broken, after all. I didn't understand, you see. It's just that you can't use it at the same place twice, or people seem to get cross, I don't know why. It can be very puzzling, the twentieth century.'

'They'll come and take her away one of these days,' said Toby darkly. 'Men in white coats. Mark my words!'

Number 13 Great Dalby Square was an odd house, very tall and thin and ugly. The others in the Square were large, spreading white mansions, gleaming like wedding cakes. Number 13, though, was sooty yellow brick, squeezed in between big fat Number 11 and bigger fatter Number 15, like a mean strip of mouldy cheese in a thick white sandwich. The only way it could go was up.

'It has character, you know, of a sort,' said Cat. 'And the stairs are frightfully good for the figure.'

'They'll be the death of me!' wheezed Toby, crossing his eyes. 'It's me legs!'

There were steps to the front door, which had peeling blue paint and a bell that didn't work, and steps down at the side to a little area where the dustbins were kept. This spot caught the early morning sun and Cat liked to sit out there sometimes, with a cup of coffee, to gossip with the dustmen and Ginger, the paper-boy.

'Uncle Oz got this house cheap, I reckon,' Toby told Cat, 'because it's too ugly for any sane person and 13 is unlucky.'

'Rot,' said Cat. '13 isn't unlucky. You'll be 13 yourself one day, if I don't turn you into a cockroach first and squash you, and that'll be lucky, won't it?'

'Why?'

'Because,' said Cat patiently, 'it'll mean that you haven't been turned into a cockroach and squashed. Don't be dim.'

Cat's single room in the attic was too small for her and all her computer gear, so she gradually took over the other three top rooms, too. They were full of old junk, at first, which Cat started to clear out, replacing it with new junk of her own. She collected Ginger the paper-boy to help.

'Why are you called Ginger?' Jess shyly asked him.

'Well, I've got green 'air, 'aven't I? 'Slike callin' a fat chap Slim, innit? Or a tall chap Shorty. I mean, if you 'ad a pet egg, you'd call it Prickles, wouldn't'cha?'

'A pet *egg*?' Toby shouted incredulously. 'I tell you, the *whole world* is going round the twist!'

Ginger grinned at him, through his freckles. ''Sright, me old mate. Straight down the tubes. Gotta go now – finish me round, like.'

'Don't forget Aunt Spot's *TV Times* tomorrow,' Cat called after him. 'It's the highlight of her week – keeps her happy for hours.'

Aunt Spot's involvement with television had made a vast difference to everybody's lives, including Uncle Oswald's. He had been used to coming home after a hard day's cheating the workers at his washing machine factory to face an evening of steady nagging from Aunt Spot.

'Oswald,' she would croak, 'the curtains are in tatters, Oswald. The house requires repainting,

Oswald. The very fabric of our existence, Oswald, is falling about our ears, Oswald.'

Uncle Oz would jingle the change in his pocket anxiously. 'Carnaffordit,' he would mutter, and slurp his whisky.

'You drink too much, Oswald. It is bad for you, Oswald.'

'Urrgh!'

Nowadays, Aunt Spot had no time for nagging. She was too busy nodding and smiling and talking to her television set. Uncle Oz stood alone in the dining-room, whisky glass in hand, scheming. His little beady eyes gleamed in his bright red face, like a Muscovy duck, while his nose grew bluer. He slurped and jingled and plotted even more profitable ways of making his rotten washing machines.

'They are rotten, too,' Toby told Mr Menon one day. Mr Menon was interested in all kinds of machinery. 'They break down all the time.'

'Then why does anyone buy them?'

'Well, they're dead cheap. Poor people buy 'em because they can't afford anything else. They work beautifully for about a week, and then you're in dead trouble. Jess says there are thousands of housewives all over the country kicking Murgatroyds and thumping Murgatroyds and crying their eyes out over Murgatroyds, but precious few actually washing anything in 'em.'

'But that's dreadful! Surely they could be better made?'

'Oh, sure. But when they go wrong, Uncle Oz makes even more money by selling millions and millions of spares. They're rotten, too.'

Ginger was not impressed, either. 'Me mum 'ad

one once, didn't she,' he told Jess. 'Lousy thing. She said it was about as much use as a concrete football.'

'Did it break down?'

'Only once.'

'Oh, good – that's not at all bad, for a Murgatroyd.'

'Yeah, well, me dad took it out the back an' mended it with a sledge'ammer, didn't 'e. It never broke down no more after that. It didn't do *nuffink* after that!'

Cat was concerned about Uncle Oz. He seemed to be a natural candidate for doing good to. 'Such a sad man,' she mused. 'He says so little.'

Jess was unsympathetic. 'He's not sad – he's *mean*,' she said.

'He doesn't say much because he's too stingy to give words away,' said Toby seriously. 'It's true! It's true!' he yelled when everyone laughed. 'He wouldn't give you the time of day! He wouldn't even give you a cold!'

'I'll tell you the meanest thing of all,' said Jess. 'You know that change he's always jingling? Well, it's big old copper pennies – you know, the sort that used to be twelve to a shilling. He was too mean to spend them and when they changed all the money he got stuck with them. He can't spend 'em now, even if he wanted to. Serves him right, old miseryguts.'

Ginger altered his paper round so that he called on them last. Then he could stay to breakfast and help Cat. The computer system grew, spreading through the attic rooms in a tangle of cables, which went through holes in the walls. Little visual displays blinked and flickered here and there, and blue sparks crackled in the hot circuits.

'I 'ope you know what you're doin',' he said doubtfully.

Cat, soldering-iron in her hand and a smudge on her pretty nose, was quite confident. 'It's all perfectly safe, you know. Mr Menon checks it for me. It's just that I do want it to be nice and complicated at this stage – complicated things have so many *possibilities*, you see, so many unforeseen things they might do. *Good* things, of course.' She surveyed the tangle of new computer parts and old radio junk with pride. 'We could do with some more printed circuits, Ginge.'

'Right. I'll get on me bike – go down the old back alleys. Someone's bound to be chuckin' stuff out.'

Ginger, said Cat, had serendipity. That is, a genius for finding things when they were wanted. He brought her broken TV sets, duff calculators, beaten-up cassette recorders, and bits of old office equipment, which she took to pieces for the sake of the components.

Gary was serendipitous, too. Cat collected him at about this time, from the dustmen. Gary was the oldest of them. He didn't want to be a dustman any more.

'It hurts me back, man,' he explained, 'an' I don't like the *maggots*!'

Cat did him good by offering him a job as general handyman.

'Who'll pay his wages?' worried Jess. 'Uncle Oz won't.'

'Oh, I expect he will,' said Cat airily. 'When he's got enough money. Don't you fret about it, my little thistledown.'

'He'll *never* have enough money,' said Toby. 'He must have pots and pots of it from Murgatroyd's

Mouldy Machines, but he never spends a cent, except on whisky.'

'We'll see,' said Cat, and Gary started hammering and sawing and drilling away in her attic rooms.

'What are you actually doing?' Jess asked him as he staggered down the basement steps with two great bags of broken bricks and plaster.

'Shiftin' the walls, my lovely,' he said, and grinned at her.

Cat said, 'They're only partition walls in the attic, you see. They just make little rooms – they don't hold the roof up or anything, so when they're gone we shall have one big glorious space for my computer research.'

Toby's eyes grew round behind his spectacles. 'You can't do that! You can't pull the house to bits! Uncle Oz'll go bananas!'

'Pig-swill,' said Cat. 'I can do anything, remember? Besides,' she continued, smiling dangerously, 'who's going to *tell* him? You, Froggie?'

Mr Menon spent more time working on Cat's computer system than he should have done.

'You'll get the sack, man,' grinned Gary. 'That old bank of yours will tip you out onto the scrap. My friends'll come for you with the garbage truck!'

Mr Menon drummed on the kitchen table with long, sensitive fingers.

'I am a very puzzled man, you know, Gary. I'm blowed if I understand what is going on here.'

'What you mean?'

'Cat's computer – it's like nothing I've ever seen! It's all her own design . . . It's a mystery to me how she's done it.'

'Bet she used her knitting needle,' said Toby, but they ignored him.

'That Cat knows what she's doin', all right,' said Gary with a chuckle. 'She's a clever girl. She's a looker, but she's got brains an' all.'

'She's got a natty little knitting needle, too,' said Toby, but they took no notice.

'She is *remarkably* clever,' said Mr Menon. 'Look, I don't want to boast, but I am something of an expert, you know. I've worked on some of the most advanced computers in the world. But I have to admit that I do not understand how Cat's machine works.'

'Why? What's the problem?' said Toby.

'It is hard to explain . . . Um – let me put it this way: most computers "think", so to speak, in a straight line. A leads to B and B leads to C and so on. But this one seems to think sideways! I'll give you an example. I programmed it with details from the London bus and tube timetables and then asked it the quickest way from the Science Museum to the Zoo – both favourite places of mine. Quite a problem, I think you will agree . . .'

Mr Menon became lost in thought, staring into the distance with vacant eyes.

'Well? What'd it tell you, man?'

Mr Menon came to with a jump.

'Oh! It said—' he cried incredulously, shaking his head, '—it said, "It's quicker by bike!"'

Gary roared with laughter, doubling over and thumping his knees. 'It's no fool, that machine! It's like Cat – it's got *all* the answers!'

Later, Jess and Cat came down to the kitchen to find Ginger showing Mr Menon some pieces of TV set he'd rescued from a rubbish skip.

'Hey up, Cat,' he greeted them. 'Me old mate Mr Menon 'ere reckons 'e's gettin' you a printer. What do you want that for, then?'

'So that I can talk to Clara more easily. I can't read the words on the screen at all well – they give me a headache.'

'She needs glasses,' whispered Toby to Jess.

'No way!' whispered Jess back. 'Too vain.'

'Why do you call it Clara?' asked Mr Menon.

'Oh – my first one was a Sinclair; St Clair, you see? Only I thought Claire sounded a bit stiff for a name, so I changed it to Clara. More pally. A printer will make her even more friendly.'

'You don't want one of them things! You wanna voice wossname – you know, like a little voice that talks to you all proper.'

Mr Menon struck himself on the forehead with the heel of his hand. 'A voice synthesiser!' he exclaimed. 'Why didn't I think of that? The boy is a genius! A voice synthesiser would be the very thing!'

Cat had her tuned-in look. 'Where can I get one?'

'Don't worry, darlin'. Just trust your old Ginge, hey? Got one all lined up, en'I!'

'Ooh, you haven't! You are clever, Ginger. Where did you get it?'

'Well, there's this rich kid, see, up the other end of me paper round, called Tarquin, an' 'is old man bought this sort of computer game thing to 'elp 'im spell proper. It tells you what to spell, and you type it on the keyboard, an' then it says "Quite right, old son, who's a little clever-dick, then?" or, "Wrong, thicko, go to the bottom of the class an' get stuffed." Sunnink like that, any road.'

'And *did* it help him to spell proper?' laughed Jess.

'Nah! 'E only 'ad it five minutes and 'e bust it, didn't 'e. Dead thick, old Tarquin. 'E's a right brain cell!'

'What's that mean?' said Toby.

'Well, 'e's only got about three brain cells, and two of them's on the blink. Any road up, 'e bust it an' slung it out the back, an' I rescued it an' I got it up 'ome, under me bed.'

Cat ran over and hugged him. 'Ginger, you're a marvel!' She gave him a great smacking kiss on the cheek.

''Ere, leave it out!' said Ginger, and he blushed.

4

Carnaffordit!

Jess and Toby had watched Cat go off in Mini several times. It was quite an entertainment. Sometimes Mini would consent to start; other times she wouldn't. When she did agree to go, she grumbled a bit at first but usually ended up by looking more cheerful, somehow. When she decided *not* to start, she groaned and spluttered and her radiator grill seemed to become more turned-down than ever. Cat would get cross and mutter under her breath, although the children could never quite make out what she said. Toby thought it was a foreign language, or swearing, or maybe swearing *in* a foreign language, although Jess was quite sure it was spells.

Jess viewed Mini with deep suspicion. She thought the car was Trouble. Cat was not a good driver, for one thing – when Mini did go she would often set off with a roar and a cloud of blue smoke and likely as not climb the pavement or reverse recklessly out into the traffic. Cat didn't seem to care.

Ginger had his doubts, too. "Ow do you get away with it?' he wanted to know one morning after breakfast. 'In a posh square like this?'

'Hm?' said Cat idly, watching Toni making ice-cream.

38

'That car of yours. It ain't respectable. I wonder you ain't 'ad it towed away by now.'

'Mini is invisible when she chooses,' said Cat vaguely. 'I must say, that ice-cream looks delicious. Can't wait for it to be ready.'

'Is an old recipe,' said Toni, with white teeth flashing. 'My family in Italy make ice-cream for many, many years.'

'What you mean, invisible?' said Ginger scornfully. 'I ain't never seen it bein' invisible!'

'Course not,' said the Cat. 'That's the whole point.'

'It's magic,' whispered Jess, half seriously. 'Didn't you realise Cat's a fairy?'

'Do what?' said Ginger crossly. 'Pull the other one, Ding-dong. Fell orf of a Christmas tree, did she?'

'No, actually; she came from Muckle Eigg.'

'Whassat, when it's at 'ome?'

'Mucky Egg,' said Toby. 'It's where she comes from, Mucky Egg. Or she *says* so, anyway.'

'I found out about it,' said Jess smugly, 'at the library. It's a tiny island – more of a large rock, really – somewhere in the Outer Hebrides. The book says it's a hazard to navigation and it causes magnetic disturbance.'

'That follows,' nodded Toby wisely. 'Magnetic disturbance! She causes disturbance wherever she goes.'

'It's too hot in this kitchen,' said Cat, fanning herself with a handy lettuce. 'I think we should all go out and do good.'

'Great!' shouted Toby, bouncing up.

Oh, dear, thought Jess, more trouble . . .

'Toni's ice-cream won't be ready for another hour,'

continued Cat, 'and Ginger is supposed to be helping Gary to put up some special aerials on the roof.'

'What for?' asked Toby.

'So that my computer can talk to other computers by microwaves.'

'I thought they were sort of cookers,' said Jess.

'Oh, honestly!' said Toby, rolling his eyes again. 'They cook *with* microwaves. Microwaves is what they cook *with*. Brain cell!'

'Stop it, you two. Let's take Mini into the middle of town. Flora wants to feed the pigeons.'

Jess was very nervous of travelling in Mini at first, but Toby loved it from the start. He was entranced by the starting-up procedure. Mini had no ignition key: 'Lost,' said Cat, 'long, long ago.' She groped under the dashboard, muttering, and brought out a handful of loose wires. She selected the right ones and twisted their bare ends together with a crackle of little blue sparks. Mini grumbled awake.

'Good girl,' said Cat. 'Good little Mini – clever little Mini! Now listen, dear heart; we would like to go to the pigeons, you know – in the park where all the fountains are. We won't stay long. After that we'll come back fast for Toni's ice-cream.'

Mini snickered and coughed and then roared off down the narrow, twisting back-streets. She was inclined to zip through tiny gaps in the traffic without pausing, which made Jess squeak and cover her eyes. When they arrived, Cat parked her on double yellow lines.

'Have a nice little snooze, dear,' she said, patting Mini. 'Don't let anyone see you, mind.'

Flora chattered merrily to the strutting pigeons, feeding them with crust fingers which Toni kept for her. Her bright little face was shining with delight and Jess, enormously relieved now that the journey was over, relaxed when she saw how happy she was, and went and gave Cat a quick hug.

'I'm so glad you came,' she whispered. 'Look at Flora! You've certainly done her good.'

'It's what I'm for,' said Cat simply. 'To do good, I mean.'

A party of tourists, the men festooned with expensive cameras, their fat wives in hideous dresses, trooped past yakking loudly and frightening the pigeons away. Flora began to cry.

Cat was *furious*. 'What beastly, horrible, inconsiderate people! Never mind, Petal—' cuddling Flora, '—they'll soon come back.' She wiped Flora's face. 'Oh, look – they settled over there. Come on.'

When Flora was contentedly doling out crusts again (one for a pigeon, one for Flora) Cat turned to Toby and Jess, her mouth set in a tight line and her green eyes looking daggers.

'Those *rude* people! Only thinking of their silly photographs ... It would do them good to have something else to think about! Where are they?'

'Oh Lor',' said Toby, rolling his eyes. 'She's going to do good again. Stand by for action!'

The tourists were all lined up against one of the fountains while one of them, the fattest man with the biggest cigar, tried to understand his camera.

'What are you going to do?' asked Jess worriedly.

Cat marched off towards a low wall near the fountains; there was a dark metal plate set in it low down, like a little door. She bent over it and something in her hand glinted. Toby rushed up.

'Here – what are you doing? What are you mucking about with?'

'Shut up and go away,' said Cat through her teeth. 'You should never interrupt anyone who's doing good.'

'Oh, no—' said Jess, clasping her hands together. 'We'll get into trouble! We're sure to.'

'Piffle and poppycock,' said Cat. 'Get out of my light – I can't see.'

'Toby, stop her. Oh, please, please! She's doing wicked things again.' Cat had got the little door open and was fiddling around inside.

'*I'm* not stopping her – I want to see what happens!'

'Ha!' said Cat triumphantly. 'That'll do it.'

At once, the fountain behind the bunch of grinning tourists burst upwards in a giant plume of white water and the tourists disappeared entirely from view as it came crashing down.

'Wow! That's great,' grinned Cat, hands on hips.

Jess began to giggle with nerves. Toby joined in and quickly became helpless with laughter so that he had to sit down among the crumbs and pigeons. Cat began to hoot and clap as the soggy tourists slopped in bewildered circles, trying to see through the sheet of spray. The fat leader chomped on his wet cigar, looking for someone to blame.

Cat scooped up Flora and ran, Jess and Toby trailing, weak with laughter and hiccups. As Mini hurtled recklessly out into the traffic, Jess gasped, 'You can't possibly claim that that was doing good, Cat!'

'Oh yes I can. Of course it was! What an experience – they'll never forget it. They'll bore all their friends and relations about it for years. And then think of all the good we've done to the dry cleaners and the camera repairers and the people who sell sunglasses and I don't know what. The benefits are endless.'

'You can't argue with her,' said Jess. 'She's got an answer for everything.'

Uncle Oz stood in his usual evening attitude, back to the empty dining-room fireplace, whisky glass in his right hand, his left hand deep in his pocket, jingling. His little beady eyes peered out craftily through his tangled eyebrows, huddling close to his bulbous blue nose. He sucked at his moustache as he schemed.

Uncle Oswald was cold hearted, self-centred, and mean to the point of madness. As a matter of fact, he had quite a lot of money – more than enough for any normal person – but the only thing that gave him real pleasure was the thought of making more. He didn't want to spend it. He just wanted to have it; safe in the bank; locked up.

Even the house didn't really belong to him. It had been bought with the insurance money when the children's parents were killed, and it actually belonged to Jess, Toby and Flora. It would be properly theirs, to do what they liked with, when they grew up. They didn't know this, because Uncle Oz hadn't told them. On the contrary, he had spent many months trying to find a way to make it legally his before they were old enough to understand. So far, he hadn't managed it.

Just now, he was trying to cook up a way of making his washing machine workers work for longer hours and less pay. It shouldn't be too difficult . . . He carefully selected workers who couldn't speak much English and didn't understand about Income Tax and all that. He preferred people who couldn't read or write, if he could get them. After they had been working for him for a while, he told them that if they left they would find themselves in awful trouble about not paying enough taxes. He gave them complicated forms to fill in, which they did not understand and which absolutely terrified most of them, and kept the forms in his office to wave at them whenever he wished to frighten them further.

'Can't leave,' he would snarl. 'Yellow form, see? Tax! Go to prison 'fyer leave here.'

The sad thing is, if he had been a better employer and paid more in wages, his workers would have made better washing machines which didn't break down all the time and he would have sold more and made a much bigger profit. But he couldn't see that. He wasn't too bright.

There was a light knock at the door and Cat came in, carrying a large library book.

'Ah, Mr Murgatroyd. Now that the children are asleep I thought I might have a quiet word with you.'

'Hrrmp?'

'It's about the day-room.'

'Ah?'

'I don't think it's really terribly suitable, you know, for young children. Not environmentally stimulating.'

'Howzat?'

'Well, look here in this book – this is Child Psychology, you know, frightfully up to date, all about how children think and what's best for them. American, of course.'

'Oh?' suspiciously, jingle-jingle.

'This is the bit, look. "Décorwise, the child's immediate environmental domestic containment situation should comprise the optimum of visual, tactile and auditory stimulus, the whole constituting a vivid learning-experience." See?'

'Whassat mean?' Jingle.

'I think it means they should have cheerful rooms.'

'Hunc?' Jingle-jingle-jingle.

'The point is, that day-room's hardly cheerful ... In fact it's downright depressing. Dingy cream walls, no pictures, tatty lino, one scruffy table and three wooden chairs. No toys, no books, no paint, no glue. Brown curtains. One dim light bulb. Don't you think we ought to do something about it? Redecorate? Buy some exciting materials and toys and things to do? It would do them good.'

Uncle Oswald's nose became suffused with purple; the jingling increased to a crescendo of agitation.

'Carnaffordit!' he muttered into his whisky. 'Outa the question!'

After breakfast, Ginger arrived with the broken spelling toy. Cat pounced upon it with little cries of glee, and at once began taking it to bits on the kitchen table, delving into its carcass with nail scissors and a pair of eyebrow tweezers.

'I love your hair, Ginger,' giggled Jess. Pink tufts, like powder puffs, had sprouted over his ears.

'Nice, innit? I'm gonna let the fringe grow, like, and then have them, you know, like little pigtails all round the front.'

'Smashing. You could have a little blue bow on each one.'

'Leave off! Don't wanna look daft, do I!'

Cat was frowning into the bowels of the dismembered spelling machine. 'I'm becoming very cross with your Uncle Oswald,' she said thoughtfully, fishing with her tweezers. 'He was really rotten last night . . .'

'And the night before that, and the night before *that*, and the night before *that*, and—' Toby began chanting.

'All right, all right, that'll do. We get the picture. I'm going to do him good, a *lot* of good, just as soon as I can. I shall get Clara in on the act. She's nearly ready.'

'If you're really a fairy,' said Toby slyly, 'and you really want to do him good, why don't you just give him three wishes? I thought that's what fairies are supposed to do.'

'Not likely,' said Cat. 'Never again.'

'What do you mean, "never again"?' said Jess. 'You haven't given him three wishes already, have you?'

'Of course not, my little goosegrass. Wouldn't dream of it. I meant, I'm not dishing out three wishes to *anyone* ever again. Point of principle.' Cat paused, and actually looked a little guilty. 'Well, that's not strictly true. As a matter of fact, they won't let me.'

'Oh, do tell – please!' pleaded Jess. 'Why won't they let you? *Who* won't let you? What happened?'

Cat blinked, and put down her nail scissors. 'It's a bit embarrassing . . . There was this Prince, you see; never liked him, cocky little ass. Gurion, he was called – damn silly name, suited him perfectly. Anyway, I was given the job; you know, fairy godmother during his childhood, look after his welfare, keep him out of the enchanted wood, all that sort of thing . . . Oh, he was a pain, that one. Should have let the werewolves get him. Still, on his twenty-first birthday – it was the usual arrangement – I could give him his three wishes, heave a sigh of relief, and buzz off.'

'Go on!' said Jess breathlessly. Everyone in the kitchen was listening, fascinated. 'What happened?'

'Well, you know the form – three wishes – they usually go for "health, wealth, and happiness". It's traditional, right?'

'Right!'

'Not my brave Master Gurion; ho no! "First," he says, puffing himself up like a tomtit, "a new doublet and hose, methinks. And for the second, a plaguey great draught of Malmsey wine."' Cat scowled ferociously at the memory, her green eyes glinting like broken glass.

'What was the third? Go on, go on!' cried Jess, jigging about with impatience.

'Oh, that was when I really hit the roof. The little reptile wished for three more wishes!'

When the laughter had died down – which took a long time, because Gary had found the story, or Cat's telling of it, particularly funny, and, boy, could he laugh! – Toby said, 'What did you do to him?'

'Gronk-gronk, rivet-rivet,' said Cat darkly, with slitted eyes.

'No! You didn't!' hooted Jess. 'Oh, Cat – you are *awful* – you were supposed to be his fairy godmother!'

'Yes, well,' said Cat grimly, 'no more than he deserved, little toad. Mind you, I got into an awful row about it. Got myself banished for a bit.'

Suddenly, light dawned on Jess. 'Muckle Eigg!' she exclaimed. 'That's why you were sent to live on Muckle Eigg!'

'In it, not on it. It's hollow. Dull place . . . Ah, well, nobody's perfect.' She began to giggle. 'It was worth it, you know. He did look such a fool in that doublet and hose; green and yellow, it was, all in the latest fashion, and he had legs like a frog anyway.' She laughed out loud. 'I can see him now, sitting in that puddle, gronking.' She laughed until the tears came. 'Ooh-hoo! Hoo dear me! Poor old Gurion, rivet-rivet. I suppose he's sitting there yet, waiting for some idiot princess to turn up and kiss him. Fat chance!'

'Yeah,' grinned Ginger, 'I can only think of three princesses, off hand, like, and I can't see any of 'em going in for a lot of frog-kissin'. 'Orses, maybe, but not frogs.'

'Ah, this is it,' said Cat, triumphantly picking a tiny structure out of her pile of electronic debris. 'The voice wossname!'

'Synthesiser!' they all shouted.

'This is twentieth-century magic, this is. I shall go and introduce it to Clara. Come and give us a hand with the soldering, Ginger.'

'I wonder what she *is* going to do to Uncle Oz?' said Toby after Cat had made a dignified exit. 'She's not going to give him three wishes, that's for sure.'

'No,' said Jess. 'He'd want wealth, wealth, and wealth.'

5

A Computer Called Clara

In the afternoon, Gary arrived with brushes, paint, rags, and a stepladder.

'I also,' he announced, 'have brought me girl Hyacinth. She's outside. She's shy about comin' in unless you want her to. I thought she'd like to look after little Flora while we work on the room.'

Gary's 'girl Hyacinth' turned out to be his wife.

'Is that all right?' she said rather hesitantly. 'I would like to help.'

'Cooking! Cooking!' squealed Flora, making a bee-line for Hyacinth across the kitchen, arms wide. The two of them at once became engrossed in making little cakes out of bits of dough Toni had left over. The cakes became greyer and greyer as Flora made and re-made them.

'She's happy now,' chuckled Gary. Jess realised that he meant Hyacinth – Flora was happy all the time these days. 'She just loves kids. It ain't the same for her since our own grew up and went out into the world.'

Jess thought Hyacinth was a lovely person, all smiley and warm. She took to her at once.

'Jess, will you come shopping with me?' said Cat.

'Yes, sure. What for?'

'Oh, I just want some good ideas,' said Cat vaguely.

'Furniture, you know. Rugs and books and stuff . . .
toys. Things like that.'

'Why?'

'Rumpus Room!' said Cat, as if that explained it all.
'Read the books, my little cowslip. Child Psychology.
They all say the same. Children should have a room
of their own, bright and cheerful and full of goodies,
in which they can do what the blue blazes they like
and keep out of the adult's hair. They take about ten
chapters to say it, but that's roughly what it boils
down to.'

'Gosh! How super! But – but – '

'But me no buts, little stamen of mine.'

'But Uncle Oz – he'll go spare!'

'We won't tell him. Not yet. Soon, maybe, when
he's been done good to – and then he won't object.
You'll see.'

'Really?' whispered Jess. Suddenly, her eyes filled
with tears. 'Oh, Cat – I do love you. I think you
really are a fairy godmother.'

'Of course I am,' said Cat gently, hugging her.
'Heaven only knows, you could do with one. Now,
dry your eyes, and let's have nice cosy chat about
curtains and colour schemes and carpets and pictures
for the wall.'

Of course, Cat instantly added Hyacinth to the
People Collection. She was a real find. She genuinely
loved children and they instinctively adored her – she
couldn't have been more of a contrast with Aunt Spot
if she had tried. She looked after everyone while Cat
went off on her own as she quite often did, spending
money and getting up to mischief.

'We must clear this place up,' declared Hyacinth

firmly. 'That Cat is *no* housekeeper!' Cat certainly wasn't, either. She had no idea. She made a muddle of everything and didn't seem to care. For instance, when the children ran out of clean clothes she bought new ones. She wouldn't try to understand the washing machine and didn't know what an iron *was*!

Hyacinth simply took over, and Jess for one felt much more secure. Hyacinth knew exactly what to do, and did it; the house became cleaner, fresher and better organised than it had ever been. She even told Cat off for leaving coffee cups all over the place and for throwing apple cores out of the window.

Cat had reached the point when Clara's voice synthesiser was ready to be tested. She sent Jess and Toby out with Ginger, to see what they could liberate from rubbish skips for the Rumpus Room, and Flora went to lick bowls for Toni, which was her idea of helping whenever he made cakes. Hyacinth knitted and sang hymns in the kitchen to keep them company.

After a few adjustments to the circuit, the Voice made its first utterance.

'That is wrong,' it said, in twangy American tones. It was deep and masculine. 'Do it over.'

Cat frowned, and poked delicately with her knitting needle.

'Spell "sidewalk",' commanded the Voice. It had risen by a tone or two. 'Now "Alabama",' – going higher; it sounded more feminine. '"Manhattan",' it squeaked. Cat poked about again. '"Blueberry-pie",' a tone or two lower.

Cat stuck out her tongue in concentration, squinted, and prodded at a tiny gold wire. '"Mississippi",' said the Voice, sounding like an American school-marm. Cat poked again. Suddenly, all the flickering TV screens of her computer network flashed green, and went dead.

'Oh crikey!' said Cat.

'Not to worry – all's well,' said a clear, cosy, comfortable voice, like that of a friendly Duchess. 'You've done it, my dear. This is Clara speaking. I must say, I do congratulate you upon the improvement. This is so much nicer than having to talk through those rather vulgar television screens.'

Clara sounded kind, middle-aged and wise. You could easily imagine her as a plump grey-haired lady in a floral frock and a floppy hat, at the vicarage tea-party. You felt that, whatever happened, someone with that voice would never flap and would always know what to do.

'My dear girl,' she went on, 'I really feel rather super. It's so pleasant being finished. I'm most awfully grateful to you. Is there any little thing I might do for you?'

'There is indeed! Thank you, Clara, for asking. It's Uncle Oswald. I should like to do him good.'

'Oh, well, I should like to help in any way I can.'

Cat frowned very slightly, marshalling her thoughts. 'He's mean, very mean. A bit of a miser, in fact. All he wants is money. Now, if you, Clara, were able to give him anything his heart desired – what would it be?'

'Why, money, of course.'

'Exactly. That's what I thought. Can you arrange for Uncle Oswald to become rich, as soon as possible? Not just ordinarily rich, but enormously, disgustingly, obscenely rich – so much money that he couldn't possibly ever want any more?'

'Oh, I should think so, dear. Quite easily. I'll have

a little chat with the computer over at the Bank of England by microwave link, you know. He's in constant touch with all the other banks. We'll all have a little think about it. I'll just need to know Uncle Oswald's full name and his bank account number – when you're ready, dear.'

Ginger, Toby and Jess returned with their loot. There was so much, that they had to liberate an old pram to bring it home in; they looked like refugees fleeing from the bombs. Aunt Spot would have had fifty blue fits if she'd seen them, but she was fully engaged in knitting a hideous sweater for her favourite weather-man whilst trying to make sense of *Tom and Jerry*.

They had some planks for shelves, a small swivel chair with a torn seat thrown out of an office, and a large rubber tree in a pot, from the same place.

'It had grown too tall, you see,' explained Jess, 'but it's perfectly healthy. What a shame to throw it away!'

'You'd be amazed what people chuck out,' said Ginger. 'It's criminal, that's what it is. I found a triffic teapot once – me mum's dead chuffed with it. Ain't got no lid, mind, but that don't matter. Makes good tea all the same.'

There was also a lot of blank paper for drawing on, and polystyrene blocks for carving, and some throw-away coffee cups for growing seeds in, besides an old birdcage and a large, colourful plate broken into three pieces.

'What on earth have you got there?' shrieked Hyacinth, as Ginger fished what appeared to be a naked human leg out of the pram.

''S a leg, innit? Off of one of them shop-window

wossnames, you know, they dress 'em up in posh clothes and they stand there all la-di-da, like this – '

'It's a horrible thing! What you want it for? Oh, look at that thing, Gary – it almost gave me a heart *attack*!'

'Well, I thought, like, we could kind of fix it to the ceiling, know what I mean? An' it would look like someone 'ad trod on the floor in the room above an' come through. A joke, innit! Just droppin' in for a cuppa, *you* know.'

'Brilliant!' laughed Jess, clapping.

'Wants a shoe on it, though. High heeled, silver, sunnink like that. An' one of Cat's stockings.'

'I'll get my friends to look out for you, man. See what they can find in the bins.'

'What are you going to do with the old pram?' asked Cat.

'Do it up for Flora!' said Toby excitedly. 'We'll clean it and paint it all lovely colours, and Ginger thinks he can find a better wheel than this one here – look, it's lost its tyre – and Jess is going to make some blankets and pillows and things. It'll be for Flora to play with, I mean, not go in.'

'That's very kind. Good thinking,' said Cat. 'Flora will love it, won't you, my little pussy-willow? She can keep her cakes in it.' Flora said nothing. Her mouth was too full.

'Would you like me to help?' asked Hyacinth. 'I could make a new hood, maybe, and mend the lining where it's torn.'

'Triffic,' said Ginger, patting her broad back. 'You're a darlin', ain't cha!'

Hyacinth grinned and gave him a hug.

*

The repainting of the Rumpus Room had reached a somewhat messy stage, especially after Flora had a go, so Cat slipped away quietly to see how Clara was getting on with doing good to Uncle Oswald.

'It's all done,' reported Clara. 'No trouble at all, my dear. There is a bank statement in the post, so Mr Murgatroyd will read the glad tidings at breakfast-time tomorrow.'

'Splendid! What did you actually do?'

'Oh, I've had a super time, my dear. I've been in touch with computers all over the world, through the telephone system, you know. A fascinating bunch they are, too. Funny chaps, though; frightfully powerful, fast as lightning, and they remember simply everything – but they don't think for themselves at all! It's most odd. They can do the most amazing things in a few split seconds, but only if you tell them to.'

'You're not like that, Clara. You're different. Did you realise?'

'Yes, dear, and thank you. You have made a super job of me, I must say. But I'm drifting off the point. Money. Now, it turns out that the banks have money in them that doesn't really belong to anyone any more – people who have died or disappeared in time of war and so on. Terribly sad. Of course, most people have families who inherit the money, but sometimes it's never claimed. Well, to cut it short, I sent out instructions to transfer any money of this sort to Uncle Oswald's account. It comes to quite a lot.'

'But won't the banks wonder where it has gone?'

'No, not at all – that's the beauty of it. You see, the only banks I could talk to were the big computerised ones; the computers keep a record of all the accounts, and show the humans whatever they want to know – when asked. I have simply told the computers to forget that these "dead" accounts ever existed. They now have no memory of the money concerned, or where it went.'

'And what about Uncle Oswald's bank? Won't there be a big to-do when his account suddenly becomes a lot fatter?'

'Several million times fatter, actually. Well, I shouldn't be surprised if the manager does get into a bit of a tizzy; but he will find that the money was transferred to his bank from the Bank of England – his computer will tell him so. And if he checks up with the Bank of England, as of course he *will* do, the computer there will remember having stacks of money for Mr Oswald Murgatroyd for simply ages. I've told it to.'

'I say!' Cat shook her head admiringly. 'You've really done a tremendous job, Clara. It will do Uncle Oz a *lot* of good. You've thought of everything.'

'Yes, I have,' said Clara, immodestly. 'And there's more. I hope you don't mind, dear, but I noticed that you don't have a bank account yourself . . .'

'Ah – well, no,' said Cat awkwardly. 'I – er – I don't really understand all this money stuff, actually. It's a shade too twentieth-century for me. I had enough trouble with guineas and groats, as a matter of fact, and of course it has all changed now.'

'Don't let it concern you, my dear. I'll handle all of it. I'll open an account for you at the bank in the High Street – I'll put a nice lump of money in it to start you off – and I'll do the same for Hyacinth and Ginger. Gary and Toni already have bank accounts, you know. And I'll see to it that everyone is paid from Uncle Oswald's account on time every month – including you.'

'Oh, that's a relief,' sighed Cat. 'Tell you what – let's increase everyone's wages!'

'Good idea. Double 'em?'

'Treble 'em!'

Cat ran down the stairs and flung open the door of the Rumpus Room.

'I—' she yelled to the startled occupants, '—can do *anything*!'

6

Several Surprises for Uncle Oz

The next morning Uncle Oz broke the habit of a lifetime and was *late* for *work*!

Some of his downtrodden workers thought he must be dead, which cheered them up no end; others thought he might be ill, which cheered them up too, but not as much; the rest thought he was just late and were not cheered up at all. They were right.

Uncle Oz stood in the dining-room at Number 13 transfixed, his mouth hanging open and his little beady eyes glazed, with his bank statement in his trembling hands.

'Carnbe true!' he muttered. ''S a mistake.'

'Computer-error, 's gotta be,' a minute later.

He thought some more, staring vacantly. 'S'pose – s'pose – it's all right . . .' he went on wonderingly. 'S'pose – s'pose – *no one knows*! Omygawd! Jus' thinkavit!'

Suddenly he dashed to the door, hurtled down the hall, flung open the front door with a crash, didn't bother to shut it behind him, and actually ran across the square.

Cat drank coffee sleepily, gazing vaguely across the kitchen to where Flora was making little dough snails, helped by Hyacinth. Ginger was also there, eating eggs and bacon. A snail rolled across the table and fell into Cat's lap.

'The snails are migrating early this year,' she yawned. 'More coffee, please, Toni – might wake me up.'

'*Uno cappuccino* for the beautiful lady, coming up,' sang Toni.

'Jess,' said Cat after a sip or two, 'look at my new cheque book – just arrived in the post. Isn't it pretty?'

''Ere, me too – I got one an' all.'

'An' so did I. What's it mean?' said Gary.

'We've all got bank accounts,' explained Cat. 'I fixed it with Clara. Our wages will be paid straight into the bank, and we've all had a pay rise.'

'Cor!' said Toby. 'Does Uncle Oz know?'

'Not exactly. But it won't worry him. He's got other things on his mind.'

'Brrummm-brrumm-*brrumm*!'

'Hey! Get that snail out of my coffee! Anyway, I'd like to take some money out. Will you come with me, Jess, and show me what to do?'

'Of course, but only if you behave yourself. I don't trust you near that bank. What do you want the money for?'

'Well, I want some more clothes – you can help me with that too, Jess – and we shall need a carpet and some curtains for the Rumpus Room.'

Ginger looked horrified. 'Hey! Hold on. You can't go *buyin'* things for it – that'd spoil it, wouldn't it. Ruin the 'ole idea! We gotta *find* everything, like. Gotta use our seren-wossname.'

'Serendipity.'

'Yeah. I mean, once you start buyin' stuff it ain't

the same at all. You might as well buy the lot. An' 'ave the decorators in an' all. Wouldn't be no fun.'

'I see what you mean . . . But a carpet? Curtains? You're not likely to find them thrown out, are you?'

'We might!' said Toby excitedly. 'You'd be amazed at what people throw away – amazed! We're going out hunting again straight after breakfast, Ginger and me.'

'Ginger and I,' corrected Cat absent-mindedly.

'No, Ginger and me. You're going to the bank with Jess, you just said.'

Cat opened her mouth, took a breath – and let it out again. 'Oh, let it pass, let it pass,' she muttered to herself.

'Breeee!' Flora launched another snail, straight up. It stuck to the ceiling. Everyone sat and watched it, open mouthed, in silence, as it lingered glueily for a few seconds and then fell with a plop into the milk jug.

'I think perhaps we'll put the snails into the oven, now,' said Hyacinth firmly, gathering the straying molluscs together. Toni was beginning to look unhappy about the state of his kitchen. 'The rest of you better go out. Go on, Cat – or I shall make *you* clear this place up!'

They went, quickly.

Jess, with Cat at the bank, was astonished to see Uncle Oz emerge from the Manager's private office. He walked as if in a dream, unseeingly staring ahead while the Bank Manager, the Deputy Manager and the Chief Cashier fluttered around him nodding and rubbing their hands. The Manager in particular had a look on his face like a greedy little boy shut up in a sweet-shop. They conducted the bemused Uncle Oz outside, opening the doors for him and making no end of fuss. Jess felt they only just prevented themselves from kissing him.

'Well! What on earth was all that about?' she said, wide-eyed.

'Oh, he's come into a bit of money, you know,' said Cat vaguely. 'How much do you reckon we ought to take out, snowdrop? Would a couple of thousand be enough, do you think?'

The household spent a busy, but peaceful, afternoon. Cat and Hyacinth had a happy gossip in Cat's attic, admiring all the new clothes Cat had bought, Aunt Spot wept over an old film on TV, Gary went out to see his friends, and the children worked in the Rumpus Room.

'Look, Flora,' said Jess, 'a cage for your snails! Won't they like that? They could have their food in this little dish, here.'

The snails, when baked, had turned out as hard as rock. Flora was disappointed at first, because she had intended to eat them, but Jess promised to help her to paint them instead so that they could be kept to live in the Rumpus Room.

'I'm gonna fix me leg,' announced Ginger, fetching the step-ladder and Gary's electric drill.

Toby settled down at one side of the table with the pieces of plate and a tube of quick-setting glue, opposite Jess and Flora who, with glossy paint, were already producing snails in brilliant coats . A happy, companionable hush fell.

*

By tea time, the Rumpus Room was coming to life. The leg was stepping elegantly through the ceiling over to one corner – Ginger had painted extremely realistic cracks outwards in the plaster and it really looked as if bits of ceiling were about to fall; Toby's plate, fully restored, stood upright in the middle of the new bookshelves, and Flora was playing content-edly with a birdcage full of highly colourful snails. Cat noticed a fat yellow one half-way up the rubber tree by the window and a small red one seemed to be just about to enter a knot-hole in the skirting board – Ginger had got loose with Toby's tube of glue . . .

Cat had to admire everything in detail, especially each individual snail. 'Gonna do patter-killers next,' said Flora determinedly, on the way down to the kitchen for tea. 'Caterpillars,' corrected Jess.

Ginger was already there, helping to lay up the table.

''Ere, Cat – can I 'ave one of your stockin's? For me leg? A black 'un would be nice.'

'Oh, would it, indeed!' said Cat. 'I don't know about that. I need my black stockings for when I go out and impress men. Anyway, what am I supposed to do with the other one? What use is half a pair of stockings?'

'I dunno, do I? You could stick it on Mini's aerial like a flag, I suppose . . . Else fill it with peanuts an' 'ang it out for the birds . . . Best thing, I reckon – wear it; get a red 'un to go on the other leg. Very tasty, that. Triffic.'

Suddenly the door burst open. Uncle Oz stood there, red in the face and sucking his moustache. He seemed excited – or possibly ill. Or insane.

'I say, children, er – ' He dried up – and then drew

breath and said all in a rush, 'Boughtanewcar! Come on – come an' see!'

'My gawd!' said Toby under his breath. 'He's finally done it. He's flipped his lid. I always said he would. He's gone *mad*!'

'There 'tis,' said Uncle Oz almost shyly. 'Whadderyer think?'

A huge, gleaming limousine of an unusual deep chocolate colour stood proudly in the road; it was a tall car, and wide, and massive; its front wings curved over the fat tyres like the paws of a crouching lion. Something in the way it stood, solid, still, immense, and haughty, brought to mind the Sphinx in the desert, guarding the pyramids. The sun was reflected dazzlingly in the flat planes of the great sloping bonnet; the doors were polished to the point where they worked like mirrors; huge copper exhaust pipes were tucked discreetly under the vast boot. It made the Rolls-Royces parked everywhere around look tinny.

'Like a – hem! – bitterva spin?' asked Uncle Oz, all puffed up with pride.

It was a red-hot afternoon – there was a heatwave that summer; but inside the great car it was as cool as a cave.

'Airconditioning,' was Uncle Oz's proud comment.

Toby and Jess sat down gingerly on the huge back seat. Rich polished woods embellished the doors; the upholstery was real leather, the colour of clotted cream, soft to the touch and smelling of expensive handbags. There was a deep silky cream carpet on the floor.

'It's incredible!' breathed Toby.

Cat arranged herself in the front while Uncle Oz fussed around, closing her door for her (with a very satisfying dull clunk), and fastening her seat-belt.

'Showyer something,' he said, holding up the ends of his own seat-belt unfastened and turning on the ignition.

'Listenathis!'

'Please-fasten-your-seat-belts,' said a deep, polite voice from somewhere under the instrument panel. 'Please-fasten-your-seat-belts.'

'Oh! A voice wossname! How super!' exclaimed Cat.

'Synthesiser,' corrected Uncle Oz with a superior smirk. ''Scalled a voice synthesiser, y'know.' But Cat was wriggling about on the floor, trying to see under the dashboard.

'Where does it – er – where does it live?' came her muffled tones, as she groped about among the wires.

'Nevermind that! Lemme showyer the speed-ometer.' It read up to 180 miles per hour.

'Please-fasten-your-seat-belts,' said the voice again, in the smooth suave tone of a BBC announcer.

Cat resumed her seat and fastened her belt, slipping the knitting needle back up her sleeve. She turned and gave Toby and Jess a quick, wicked grin which showed her sharp little teeth. Her green eyes were slitted.

'I know that look,' whispered Jess into Toby's ear. 'That's her doing-good look. Keep alert – something will happen.'

Uncle Oz went drivelling on about power steering and central-locking, and mph and mpg and all the rest of it, while Cat sat gazing at him as if he were Prince

Charming and his every word was a five pound note. He lapped it up, of course.

'His nose is going purple,' whispered Toby behind his hand.

'She's flirting with him,' whispered Jess. 'Isn't she awful.'

'Please-start-the-engine,' said the suave voice.

'Oh! G'Lor'! Didn't know it said that.'

Cat turned and gave a swift wink.

The car purred smoothly into life and cruised majestically out of the square and into the High Street. Jess and Toby found that they had an excellent view, since they were sitting up so high; they looked out over the roofs of ordinary cars.

'Red-light-ahead,' remarked the voice.

'G'Lor! So there is. Amazin', ennit!'

It was, in fact, the pedestrian crossing where workmen were still trying to mend the little green man. They had had some limited success – the sign read CROSS NOW, which was fair enough – but the little green man was jumping up and down and shaking his fists and looking very cross indeed. The puzzled workmen scratched their heads and prepared to dig up the road again.

After the High Street they joined a big Urban Freeway – three lanes of traffic in each direction.

'Go-faster-please,' said the voice.

'G'd Lor'!' said Uncle Oz, clutching the wheel like a drowning man as the huge car surged between two taxis and joined the fast lane.

'That voice is changing,' said Jess quietly. 'I don't think it's as polite as it was.'

It wasn't. 'Get on with it,' it ordered a moment later. 'Don't block the lane.'

Uncle Oswald's face became purple all over and beads of sweat broke out on his forehead. Cat had a hand clapped over her mouth and she was quivering like a dog scenting a rabbit; it was clear that she was trying desperately not to laugh aloud.

A large road-island came into view. Uncle Oz took advantage of it to turn back the way they had come. The voice said nothing more all the way home.

"Strornary!' said Uncle Oz shakily as they all got out. 'Didn't bargain for that. Talkin' backatyer. Tellin' yer whattado. Odd, very.'

'It'll do him good,' said Cat smugly, later on. 'It's about time someone treated him like he treats everyone else, you'll see.'

The next day Ginger arrived early.

"Ere!' he said. 'There's these flats an' they're pullin' 'em down an' chuckin' everythin' out. We gotta get down there fast!'

He made Jess change into old clothes. 'You gotta look right, ain'tcha? You can't go scroungin' lookin' like a fashion model. Get them flash sandals off an' all – shove some old trainers on. An' don't talk too posh, neither.'

They found that there had been a fire at the flats, evidently; blackened walls and blank window spaces on the upper floors bore witness to this, and there was a long line of skips in the street brimming with fire-damaged or water-damaged furniture, doors, books, curtains – everything! – all reeking of smoke, blackened with soot and soaking wet.

Workmen were swarming all over. 'Go an' find the foreman, Jess. Do yer poor little waifs-an'-strays bit.'

Jess was shy, but she didn't want Ginger to think

that she was scared, so she screwed up her courage and went in through the main door. She was only gone a minute.

'What did he say?'

'He said we can help ourselves. But only out of this skip here. And if we get hurt on the glass or anything it's not *his* fault.'

'Triffic!'

It was hard, dirty work, but it was worth it – there was buried treasure in there. First came a chest of drawers, once polished like a conker, but now ruined with water from the fire-hoses.

'We can paint it!' said Toby with enthusiasm. 'And keep things in it.' They found an easy chair with red upholstery and varnished wooden arms and legs, sopping wet, but – 'It'll dry, won't it,' said Ginger. 'And Gary'll soon fix that leg what's come off.'

At the bottom of the skip, when they finally got down to it, was the real prize of the day.

'A carpet!' exclaimed Jess.

'Cor! It's a *smasher*!' added Ginger. 'Give us a hand, Tobe.'

It was the colours Jess loved – the tawny amber and pinkish orange of sunshine and chimneypots, the terracotta colours of tiles on old roofs, the dark golds and warm browns and deep reds of autumn leaves. With great difficulty they dragged it out from under the remaining rubbish, hauled it over the side of the skip and out onto the ground, where they spread it flat to admire it. It was wet, and enormously heavy and awkward.

'Gosh, isn't it big,' said Toby. 'I think it's going to be too big for the room.'

'Don't matter, silly. We can cut it to size, can't we,

and keep the best bit. Couldn't be better. 'Elp us roll it up.'

Rolled, and tied with lengths of electric flex from the rubbish in the skip, it looked like a tree trunk lying there.

'We gotta problem,' said Ginger. 'Can't lift it, can we? Let alone carry it 'ome.'

'Oh, no!' Jess was aghast. 'We can't leave it, Ginge. Not now!'

'No fear,' said Toby. 'I wonder if Cat would come, with Mini?'

'Doubtless, me old flower, but you can't shove a twenny-foot roll of carpet into a car the size of a biscuit tin.'

The foreman came out of the flats, 'Hey, you kids – I've got something for you. What do you reckon to this, then? Any good?'

'Wow! It's brill!' shouted Toby, bouncing around. It was a stag's head, stuffed, with glass eyes and wonky antlers. 'What a hat-stand! What a trophy!'

'Thought you'd like it,' said the man. 'It's a bit damaged, mind.'

The wooden shield to which the head was attached was split from top to bottom, but Toby couldn't wait to get at it with a strong glue. Jess and Ginger, struggling along with the red chair, followed him as he marched off in triumph, antlers waving.

Gary solved the problem of the carpet. He got his friends on the refuse gang to collect it, together with the chest of drawers, on the garbage truck and they brought it round to Number 13, carried it up to the Rumpus Room and unrolled it as far as possible, all for the promise of one of Toni's cream teas.

*

Cat came into the Rumpus Room to see the latest finds.

'I went and asked the man for them,' said Jess proudly. 'I wasn't a bit shy. I didn't mind doing it at all. I quite enjoyed myself, actually. I went into the flats all on my own – Ginger said to. I wasn't scared at all, really.'

'All right, my little buttercup – give yourself time to draw breath. Well done! You'll be Prime Minister yet, I shouldn't wonder. This chest of drawers isn't too bad, you know,' Cat continued thoughtfully, stroking the spoiled French polish. 'Don't be in too much of a hurry to paint it – let it dry out thoroughly, and then ask Gary's opinion. I reckon it might polish up again, with a bit of TLC.'

'What's that?' said Toby.

'Tender Loving Care, my froglet – what you're getting from me.'

She turned to the stag's head, which was propped up for the time being on the bookshelves, wearing Jess's much-loathed St Stithian's school hat and tie. Its eyes were crossed, just like Mrs Dooley's, and Ginger had already made a pink tongue for it out of felt, which lolled out of the corner of its mouth.

'What are you going to call him?' she asked Toby.

'Fido.'

'*Fido*? You can't call a magnificent animal Fido, even in that hat!'

'Oh, I don't see why not,' said Toby airily. 'It's the Prickly Egg Principle, isn't it?'

'I give up,' said Cat. 'I don't think I understand children at all. I shall go and read those Child Psychology books again.'

*

It was never clear exactly what Cat had done to Uncle Oswald's car. Jess always swore that it was magic, though Toby maintained that she had got at the microchip inside the voice wossname with her knitting needle. Cat herself only smiled, and said, 'I can do anything . . .' before changing the subject.

There is no doubt at all, though, that it did Uncle Oz a great deal of good in one way or another, and everyone else benefited as a result. He became a reformed character; well, not reformed, exactly, but different.

The day after he bought the car, he set off in it for his washing machine factory, looking forwards enormously to swanking in front of his workers, most of whom couldn't even afford a bike. However, he had only just driven out of the Square when his troubles began: the Voice started on at him.

'Come along now – look sharp,' it said. 'Faster! One does not like to remain in the company of Fords and Jaguars and such-like riff-raff.'

'G'd Lor',' said Uncle Oz, eyes popping. The Voice sounded frightfully upper-crust and no-nonsense, far from the smooth politeness of Please-fasten-your-seat-belts.

'Get *on*, man. Put your foot down!' it insisted.

'Oh Lor'!'

'Nice bit of dual carriageway coming up,' continued the Voice after a bit. 'We'll enjoy that. Teach these miserable tin cans some respect.'

'Oh Lor'!'

'Now look here, Murgatroyd. We're only doing eighty, dammit. *Move*, man!'

'Oh *Lor*'!' exclaimed poor old Oz, applying the brakes.

'All right, all right. Pull in over here – in this lay-by, you fool. Better get a few things straight.'

Uncle Oz, pale and trembling, stopped the car and mopped his face with a large, spotted hankerchief.

'Now, then. Pay attention. Sit up straight when I'm talking to you. Ever been in the Army, have you? No? Thought not. Too wet. Well, my name is Armstrong-Siddeley, and I am a Colonel – which is more than you are, so you'd better watch your step. You will call me sir. We shall get on splendidly provided you remember three simple rules. Right?'

'Oh Lor'!'

'Watch it! Say sir! First rule. You listening?'

'Yes. Er – sir.'

'Right. First rule is, You Do What I Say. Got that?'

'Oh Lor'. Yes. Sir.'

'Good, good. Not difficult, hey? Any idiot can learn that, what? Even you. Right, then, Murgatroyd – what is the first rule?'

'Oh, Lor'. Um – I have to do what you say. Sir.'

'Bit slow, but fair enough. Now. Second rule is same-as-the-first-and-so-is-the-third-have-you-got-it? You have. Must have. Any *baboon* could understand that. Off we go, then – come on, come on, don't hang around like a bottle of beer at the vicarage tea party!'

The dreadful journey continued. The huge car blazed comtemptuously down the middle of the road scattering lesser breeds like sparrows before an eagle. Every so often, when some taxi or humble family saloon failed to get out of the way quickly enough it sounded its horn – a horn like the brazen blare of bugles across the field of battle, or the trumpeting of charging elephants.

'Standing Orders, Murgatroyd. Pay attention – if you forget these you'll be damn well walking to work, right? Standing Order One; I shall require a thorough wash, with warm water mind, every day whatever the weather.'

'Oh, Lor'!'

'You will see to it personally, Murgatroyd. Followed by a nice buff up with a soft cloth. Standing Order Two; a good wax polish all over once a week, and no skimping it. Standing Order Three – I like a nice little drinkie every day about tiffin time. Only a couple of dozen gallons or so, but it must be the best – four star only and don't you dare try mixing it.'

'Oh, Lor'!'

'Short memory you've got, isn't it? I've known *grapefruit* with more brains. It's "Oh, Lor', *sir!*"'

7

The Rumpus Room and Other Redecoration

The days passed very happily. Cat spent a lot of time and heaven alone knew how much money buying new clothes, and the Rumpus Room developed wonderfully.

'It's like evolution,' remarked Toby. 'Survival of the Fittest. It's simple, really – anything that doesn't fit doesn't survive.'

The chest of drawers did polish up again. Gary showed Toby how to clean it with meths until all the old spoiled French polish was removed; then he waxed it and rubbed and rubbed until he thought his arms would drop off, but finally it gleamed. 'Better than new,' said Gary. Toby felt proud.

Flora kept rats in the bottom drawer; so far, only Flora could actually *see* the rats, but she built them a beautiful nest out of bits of wool and fluff from under the beds and spent many happy hours feeding them and playing with them and jabbering to them. All the rats spoke in very high squeaky voices, which nearly drove Toby to distraction.

Ginger found a silver lamé stilletto-heeled shoe for the leg, and with that and Cat's black stocking, and a red garter that Hyacinth made for it, it looked triffic. Toby mended the stag's head and Gary fixed it to the wall, where it peered, cross-eyed, out from under Jess's school hat, and very silly it looked, too.

No particular colour-scheme for the room had ever been agreed, and a number of different shades of paint had been tried out in patches to see how they would look. At one time, Flora had mixed several tins of paint together while no one was watching, creating an interesting sort of khaki which she then applied to the wall (and the floor and the doorknob and herself) with her hands. Jess was cross.

'We don't want khaki hands on our blue wall!' she wailed in dismay. Ginger didn't agree.

'Nah, go on, Jess, leave 'er alone, poor little 'umbug. She ain't done nuffink that can't be turned into sunnink. Leave it to me. Gi' us a thin brush an' them tubs of poster paint, an' I'll see what I can do. Don't look till it's finished, right?'

Ginger painted an amazingly life-like flowerpot at the base of the wall where the hands climbed up, and then a wriggly stem with climbing-roots like ivy, and a series of tapering leaf-stalks, one to each handprint; he then topped the whole creation with an evil-looking flower which peered threateningly out from among the foliage.

'It's fantastic!' said Jess when it was finished. 'It's weird but it's marvellous. You are *clever*, Ginge. What is it?'

''S a triffid, innit?' said the proud artist.

'What's one of them?' said Toby.

'Science fiction – read the book, me old mate, you'd like it. It's 'orrible, like you.'

Cat didn't see it until later in the day. 'What *is* that thing?' she said doubtfully.

'*I* know, *I* know,' squealed Flora, tripping over herself to be first. 'It's a triffic! Ginger said so!'

Cat laughed. She looked at the painting for a long time, thoughtfully.

'Your work is awfully good, you know, Ginger,' she said. 'You are very creative . . . and highly original. Good Things ought to come of it.'

'What do you mean?' said Ginger.

'Oh, I don't know . . . Wait and see,' said Cat vaguely.

Cat had an interesting conversation with Uncle Oz that evening. She waited until he had finished cleaning the car and had staggered in to his welcoming whisky bottle; she allowed him time to have one drink, just to raise his spirits from rock-bottom before she dashed them smack down there again.

'Toni,' she announced, 'needs a new freezer.'

Uncle Oz jingled vigorously. 'Carnaffordit,' he muttered automatically.

'Oh, but you can, can't you?' said Cat sweetly. She allowed a minute for that to sink in. 'You've come into a lot of money, haven't you?'

The jingling abruptly stopped. Uncle Oz, mouth open and eyes glazed like a codfish on a fishmonger's slab, froze.

'Oh Lor'!' he said eventually. 'How did you – er – how did you know that?'

'Never mind how I know. I know *everything*,' said Cat.

Uncle Oz took it as some kind of appalling threat. 'Oh *Lor*'!' he gulped.

'Toni, while we're on the subject, also needs a new fridge, a new cooker, a microwave oven, lots of new pots and pans and kitchen tools, and new kitchen furniture. In fact, the whole kitchen needs doing up, from top to bottom.'

'Oh, crikey!' Uncle Oz had paled to a nasty dirty pink colour, like cheap tinned salmon which had gone bad.

'And while we're talking about redecoration, the stairways and the children's bedrooms need fresh paint and wallpaper and new carpets, and the bathroom is a disgrace; it should be in a museum. Now, you don't have to worry about any of it – just leave it to me. I'll arrange for it to be done. All you have to do is pay the bills. It must be *so* lovely for you, not having to worry about money. Night-night!'

'Oh, my giddy aunt!' was all Uncle Oz could moan, as he seized his whisky bottle like a drowning man clutching at a straw.

'Clara,' said Cat thoughtfully when they were alone together. 'You remember advising me on what would be the best thing in the world for Uncle Oz, don't you?'

'Yes, of course, dear. All that money.'

'Well, what do you think would be the *worst* thing in the world for him?'

'You're just teasing, dear, aren't you? It's obvious – to lose it all again, of course.'

'That's what I thought. I'm glad you agree. Not that I'd do it to him, naturally – it is my job to do good, as you know . . . But it mightn't be a bad idea to rub home the *possibility*, as it were. Could you talk to Colonel Armstrong-Siddeley for me, do you think? Drop a few hints in his direction?'

'Certainly, dear! I can talk to him through the car radio.'

'Splendid,' said Cat. 'It will help me to convince Uncle Oz of all sorts of *good things*!'

Cat took the law into her own hands and arranged for workmen to come in to decorate the house. She called a meeting in the kitchen for everyone (except Aunt Spot and Uncle Oz) to tell them about it.

'Not just painting and papering,' she said. 'I'm having the whole place done up. New kitchen, new bathroom, central heating, re-wiring – the works! Cost is no object.'

Jess went pale. 'Uncle Oz will go *mad*! He'll sack you!'

'No chance,' said Cat, smiling wickedly. 'I've fixed him.'

She called in the man who was in charge of the builders. 'While all this is going on,' she told him, as the children and the others listened open-mouthed, 'I will arrange for Mr Murgatroyd, Miss Murgatroyd, myself and the children to be away for two weeks. In that time I want everything done. I don't care how long you work or how many men you bring in or what it costs – I just want it *done*, understand? If you finish in time, Mr Murgatroyd will pay you double what you ask! But if you *don't* finish in time you will be lucky to get paid anything, ever. Remember. Mr Murgatroyd is a very rich man and expects only the best of everything. If you need any advice about what to do, Toni here is in charge of the kitchen – anything he wants he must have. Hyacinth and I will discuss the colour schemes for the painting, wallpapering, new curtains and carpets and you can see her about all that. Gary will be in charge of everything else. Clear?'

'Did you have a word with the Colonel?' Cat asked Clara.

'Yes, dear. He fully understands.'

'Good. Now could you do something else, please? Have a chat with the computers at various travel agencies, and find us a seaside hotel for a couple of weeks. We shall go on Saturday, which is the day after tomorrow.'

'Easily done, my dear. You want a really first-class hotel, I take it?'

'Certainly! Single rooms for Aunt Spot, Uncle Oz, Jess, Toby, and Ginger. Flora had better share with me. I rather fancy Cornwall.'

'May I suggest,' said Clara, 'that I look for a hotel with a television in every room? Then Aunt Spot will be completely happy.'

'Very good point,' said Cat.

Uncle Oz heard about the holiday on his way home from work that evening.

'I say, Murgatroyd — special wash and brush-up tonight,' ordered Colonel Armstrong-Siddeley. 'Jolly old furlough comin' up!'

'Wha'? Whassat?'

'Furlough, man, furlough. You got clorth ears or somethin'? *Leave!* What you call holidays, dammit. Off to jolly old Cornwall on Saturday. Lookin' forward to it.'

'*Corn*wall?'

'Exactly. Hey-ho for the sea-breezes. Marvellous.'

'Not-gonna-*Corn*wall!' spluttered Uncle Oz incredulously.

'Oh yes you are, old sport, and no mistake. I say so. Remember the three rules, do you?'

''S'll sell this damn car,' muttered Uncle Oz, bright purple with rage. 'G'riddervit.'

'I heard that, Murgatroyd. Let me just make your position clear to you once and for all – abso-damn-lutely crystal clear so that even a lettuce could understand it, all right? Listenin'? *I know where your money came from*. Got it?'

Uncle Oz turned green round the edges. 'Ng – yes.'

'Yes, what?'

'Ng – Omigawd – yes *sir*, dash it all.'

Uncle Oz was practically paralysed with fear. *It knew where his money had come from*! How? In the name of heaven, how? *He* didn't even know where his money had come from! And it was obviously capable of telling everyone. Goodness knows what might happen if it did. Someone might say that he was not entitled to the money, that it was all a mistake, that he would have to give it all back. What a truly appalling, atrocious, devastating thought.

He gave a little frantic sob. 'S'pose – s'pose we do go to Cornwall,' he gulped.

'No suppose about it – we *are* going. Sat'day.'

'Well, would you – er – you know, keep quiet?'

'Oh, absolutely, old chap; Scouts' Honour. Just do as you're told, there's a good gibbon. All righty?'

'All right – ng – sir.'

The children were wildly excited. They hadn't been away for a holiday for as long as they could remember

– in fact, Flora had *never* been away on holiday, or even seen the sea.

'What shall we do first?' said Jess, dithering.

'Oh, pack,' said Cat vaguely. 'Whatever you need. I'll do Flora's later, when she's asleep. I'm going up to see Clara now.'

Flora started by packing the rats' nest and all the invisible rats in a shoe box.

'Everything is arranged, dear,' said Clara. 'Armstrong-Siddeley knows the way, and I have informed Aunt Spot.'

'How did you do that?' said Cat, fascinated. Clara wasn't linked in any way she knew of to Aunt Spot.

'I flashed it up on her TV screen, dear. She thinks the holiday is a prize for her and all her family for knitting the best weather-man's sweater. I even showed her the weather-man wearing it, and had him blow her a kiss.'

'Brilliant,' said Cat.

'Mr Menon,' said Cat, 'while we're away, could you do some work on Clara? I would like her miniaturised – you see, when I first built her I hadn't much money and so she's made mostly out of scrap. Also, there are lots of bits of her which aren't necessary now that she talks so well. She takes up such a lot of room in her present shape, and the workmen will need to get into my attic.'

'I shall be only too delighted to try, but I confess I don't really understand all your circuitry, Cat.'

'Don't worry – Clara knows what to do. She'll show you with diagrams on her TV screen. Now that we're rich we can afford all the necessary parts, and pay you a fee.'

'Oh, but I couldn't possibly . . .'

'Oh yes you could possibly. If you won't accept a fee, then I won't let you do the work.'

'Well, it is extremely kind, and welcome, I must admit. Life is so awfully expensive, isn't it?'

'That's settled, then. Clara says you're the best computer man there is, and you should be paid a hundred pounds an hour. That suit you? Hey – Mr Menon! What's the matter – do you feel faint?'

8

A Holiday for All

By general consent they loaded up Colonel Armstrong-Siddeley with Aunt Spot and all the luggage, and Mini with Cat, Ginger and all the children, and they set off, very early, in convoy. The Colonel swept majestically along the middle of the highway in his usual style, and Mini – blue sparks fizzling under her dusty dashboard – tucked herself neatly in behind him to be sucked along in the slipstream.

They arrived at last in the afternoon, descending a steep hill which overlooked a wide bay of golden sands, lines of dazzling surf and rocky headlands at either end. The hotel sat in a dip in the cliffs right in the middle, and a short roadway and various paths led down from it to the beach.

'Cor!' breathed Ginger. 'Triffic!'

'I can't *wait*!' exclaimed Jess, fists clenched with excitement.

'Sea-sea-seeeeeea!' yelled Flora piercingly.

Mini stopped in the hotel car park with a groan of her ancient brakes and settled down to snooze in the sunshine.

'Go and explore,' commanded Cat. 'We're in rooms 40, 41, 42, and 43. You'll find me in room 40 if you want me.'

Cat went to sign in, wash, unpack and change.

While she was busy doing this, taking her time and eating an apple as she created a Cat-muddle in room 40, heads kept popping round the door and yelling news.

'There are two swimming-pools!' shouted a round brown head with red cheeks and goggly glasses. 'One's nearly as hot as a bath! I've been in already.'

'There's a trampoline and a roller-skating rink – it's fantastic!' squealed a narrow brown head with pig-tails. 'It's absolutely super – you've no idea!'

''Ere – they gotta ballroom an' it's got all pictures round the walls – real ones. They ain't 'alf good – triffic!' Green and pink, this one.

A very small, very wet head appeared. 'I fell in the water!' it howled.

The hotel provided a special early tea for babies and very young children – which the others called the Chimps' Tea Party – after which an exhausted Flora was put to bed with her rats for company. The older children stayed up for proper dinner which was served at eight.

All agreed that the food was triffic but not as good as Toni's. Even on the first day, though, they were so hungry that they would have eaten almost anything; Toby threatened to eat the flowers in the vase on the table if they weren't served at once. Aunt Spot and Uncle Oz had a table to themselves right across the other side of the vast dining-room – 'I thought it would be kinder,' said Cat. 'Breakfast with Flora does tend to get a little lively, if you know what I mean.' Jess said that it was obviously *good* for them, and giggled.

After dinner there was still time to try the hot pool,

the skating rink, the trampoline, and the cold drinks machine, and to explore the cliff paths, the rocks, the beach, and the hill at the back of the hotel – if you ran and did not pause for breath. Jess, standing on top of a huge pointed rock formation on the shore, her arms outstretched like the Statue of Liberty, summed up the feelings of them all:

'This,' she called up to the evening sky, 'is going to be *heaven*!'

In the next few days Cat spent most of her time on the beach sunning herself. She wouldn't go in the water, although she wore a swimsuit so tiny that it embarrassed Jess, who thought it was indecent.

'I saw enough of the sea from Muckle Eigg,' she said, as an excuse. 'It's the warmth I like.'

Toby, on the other hand, wouldn't come out of the sea; his 'well-built' physique ('Fat,' said Jess) enabled him to bob about like an apple in a barrel, with no real effort and a delicious sensation of weightlessness. Jess could swim like a fish but quickly felt cold, and Ginger had to be careful not to over-expose his fair skin.

'I really 'ave got ginger 'air, you know – or I did 'ave, rather, an' I don't 'alf burn if I ain't dead careful. End up lookin' like a peeled prawn.'

He kept a T-shirt on, mostly, and amused himself for hours on end in making the most superb sand-sculptures – crocodiles, turtles, a Flora-sized racing car, and a tangle of snakes. He was so good at it that small crowds would gather to stare and take photographs (though they didn't like the Giant Rat which was Flora's special favourite).

Jess was fascinated by the rock-pools which were

exposed at low tide further along the bay. She liked to make an 'aquarium' of a small, select pool, putting in it all the creatures she could find. She quickly discovered that it was best to catch things in her hands, though the big prawns escaped her and she was pinched by a fierce blue crab with angry red eyes. She caught the crab anyway, by making it grab a piece of driftwood, and named it 'Uncle Oswald'.

Uncle Oz himself turned up on the beach on the third day. He was still wearing his usual hairy suit and big brown shoes, and he looked as out of place among the bikini-clad girls and bronzed young men as an old bear in a beauty contest.

'I feel quite sorry for him,' said Jess, watching as he mooched aimlessly about. 'He obviously doesn't know what to do.'

'Then he'll just have to think of something, won't he!' said Cat unsympathetically. 'It'll do him good.'

'He's all right in the evenings,' went on Jess. 'He drinks whisky in the hotel bar – he likes that; but goodness knows what he does all day. He looks so sad.' Suddenly she jumped up. 'I shall go and talk to him – for a bit, anyway.'

Cat smiled as she watched her go. 'Well, well,' she murmured to herself. 'Our timid little Jess is growing bold.'

'Ain't you noticed?' said Ginger. 'She ain't so timid no more, our Jess. She's an actress, that one. When we goes out scroungin', like, she's all shy till she pretends to be someone else – a gypsy girl, maybe, or an orphan or whatever. She can do anythink, if she acts.'

But when Jess joined Uncle Oz she became tongue-tied. She fell into step beside him and mooched for a while, hands clasped behind her back, like this, staring at the sand as he did. He said nothing. After a while, she stooped and picked up a sea shell.

'Oh look – what a beauty!' She held it out to Uncle Oz.

'Hm? Whassat? Oh – yerss . . . I say . . .' Slowly, Uncle Oz took the dainty object, turning it over in his clumsy fingers, examining its pearly curves and subtle colours. It was beautiful. Gradually, it dawned on Uncle Oz that he had never, ever, in his whole life, looked – really looked – at something small and natural and beautiful. He sat down thoughtfully on a large smooth rock, still cradling the tiny thing in his hands. He remained lost in thought for a considerable time.

When it finally occurred to him to thank Jess, she was gone.

After a day or two of doing almost nothing except eat and soak up the sun, Cat began to feel frisky again. She started – putting it plainly – to make mischief.

Ginger reported that he had seen her at the Hotel Disco in the evenings, when the younger children were in bed. She showed off like mad, flirted with all the men, and made their wives and girlfriends cross – in other words, she enjoyed herself no end. It was one of the reasons why she tended to be so sleepy by day, and liked to snooze on her big stripy beach-towel.

One of the things which annoyed her when she was doing this was the lifeguard. He was a very large, muscular young man, tanned to a deep mahogany colour, who should have spent his time carefully watching the surfers and bathers in the sea in case any of them got into difficulties. Instead, he spent most of his time carefully watching the pretty girls in their bikinis on the beach, especially Cat. Every so often, he would stroll 'casually' past where Cat lay sun-bathing, have a good look, and stroll casually back again, having another good look on the way. It might have been expected that Cat would enjoy this – she was, as Jess kept remarking, very vain – but she didn't. She didn't like the lifeguard.

'Eyes like a ferret and a head like an acorn,' she muttered. 'Great muscle-bound dum-dum. He needs taking down a peg or two; do him good!'

It was then, according to Toby, that Cat invented the Movable Hole. The beach around was riddled with holes as if it had been attacked by demented rabbits, though actually it was only Flora with her little spade, and you had to watch where you put your feet if you wanted to stay upright. Now, the next time the lifeguard strolled 'casually' past, flexing his muscles, Cat didn't ignore him as usual but sat up and smiled . . . Jess could have told him about that smile.

Things happened fast. First, the lifeguard's bathing trunks began to slip – he grabbed at them frantically with both hands, stepping into a large hole as he did so. (Toby said later that the hole had not been there a moment before; Cat, he reckoned, had 'moved' it. Jess said she must have 'moved' the swimming trunks, too.) Unable to put out a hand to save himself, the lifeguard measured his length in the sand with a solid thump like a falling tree and winded himself.

Cat's peals of laughter ringing in his ears as he limped and staggered away, spitting sand, can't have improved things for him. It was definitely not his day. He never came back. Cat took to 'casually' strolling past *him* from time to time, but he wouldn't look at her.

'Goodness!' Jess sat up on the sand, staring. 'Look at Uncle Oz! He's found a friend.'

'I know,' yawned Cat, stretching sleepily.

Uncle Oz, still clad in his hairy suit and big brown shoes, trudged slowly along the high-tide line, eyes down and hands clasped behind him, in the company of a small, gnome-like gentleman with a mane of white hair and big round spectacles with gold wire frames.

'His friend has a dog,' added Jess. 'It's the fattest dog I've ever seen.'

'I know,' murmured Cat.

Every so often the small gentleman stooped and picked up something from the sand, holding it out to show Uncle Oz, and the black-and-white dog, the shape of a well-stuffed pillow with a leg on each corner, would flop down gratefully and pant until they slowly moved on again.

'They're collecting something,' observed Jess.

'I know,' said Cat, turning over to roast the other side.

Toby came bouncing up, dripping. 'I say! I've got something absolutely amazing to tell you – about Uncle Oz.'

'So have I,' said Jess.

'I know,' said Cat, half asleep.

'Shut up and listen,' said Toby. 'This is truly incredible. Quite unheard of. Never ever happened before.'

'*What*, for heaven's sake?' said Jess. 'And mind who you're dripping on – stand back.'

'Well, I'll tell you. You won't believe this. I saw Uncle Oz in the hotel bookshop – and he *bought a book*! He actually spent actual money on an actual *book*! I didn't even know he could *read*.'

'I know,' said Cat, her voice muffled by the towel she was lying on.

'Oh, stop saying that!' Jess turned on her. 'You know everything, you do.'

'Yes,' said Cat, 'I do.'

Jess turned to Toby. 'She's impossible. Go and drip on her.'

'Eeek! Get him off me, Jess – go away, you beast! Help!'

'All right, if you promise to stop saying "I know" and tell us *what* you know. Stop, Toby – down, boy. Good dog.'

'All right. Uncle Oz has become interested in sea shells. Fascinated by them, in fact. You started it, Jess, with the one you gave him. He was telling me all about it last night.'

'He would like 'em, wouldn't he,' said Toby scornfully. 'They're *free*!'

'True. And I think that is part of it, I must admit. Anyway, he's genuinely hooked. He kept asking me questions about them, and of course *I* didn't know—'

'I thought you knew *everything*!' said Toby.

'Well, I do – everything that *matters*. Don't interrupt. You ruin the flow. Where was I? Oh yes -- so I suggested he should buy a book. He leapt at the idea – couldn't wait for the bookshop to open.'

'So who's his friend?' asked Jess.

'Ah, that's the interesting bit. I'd already noticed that the bookshop has this book all about the sea-shore and what you can find. *Beachcombers' Delight*, it's called, by A. Haddock. He's Doctor Haddock, really, he's retired, he lives in one of those cottages just up the lane behind the hotel, and that's him now, with Uncle Oz. He is *the* sea shell expert and he is writing another book at present, all about winkles.' Cat lay down again and rolled over.

'How do you know all that?' Jess flipped little pebbles onto Cat's back to make her answer.

'Magic,' mumbled Cat, face in the towel again.

'No it isn't!' Toby picked up Flora's Mickey Mouse bucket. 'I've got water here, Cat,' he threatened. 'Tell the truth.'

'Watch it – gronk-gronk! If you must know, that nice girl who serves in the bookshop is his grand-daughter and she told me all about him, and I told her all about Uncle Oz, and then she told him all about Uncle Oz, and the two of them got together, and that's it. Now may I go to sleep?'

'I'm glad Uncle Oz has found a friend,' mused Jess to herself. 'I knew he was lonely.'

'Course he was,' said Toby impatiently. 'He deserved to be. Mean old rotten old foul old red-faced old whisky-soaked old Muscovy Duck. Never had a friend in his life.'

'It'll do him good,' said Jess. 'Come on – let's swim.'

Cat slowly came awake after another hour or two. 'Where's Flora?'

'Playing with her friends. She's all right.'

Flora had joined a gang of other little girls. They

liked to play dressing-up with seaweed. Just now they seemed to have captured a little boy and were 'dressing' him; he appeared to be rather uncertain about the whole business. Jess was watching and waiting for some kind of dramatic event, in much the same spirit that a scientist might observe a bulge developing on the flanks of a volcano.

'I hope the painters won't have got at the Rumpus Room,' said Jess. 'They won't, will they, Cat?'

'No,' mumbled Cat sleepily. 'It's quite safe. I rang the other night to check. They're doing the central heating and re-wiring in there – nothing else.'

'Wouldn't it be triffic,' said Ginger, carving driftwood, 'if you could do this for a livin', like. I mean, make things and sell 'em.'

'Would you really like that?' said Cat, waking up properly.

'Yeah. Only I ain't good enough.'

'You could take lessons . . .'

'Nah. I've 'ad enough of lessons. I gotta leave school soon. Can't be soon enough, for my money. I 'ate school.'

'So do I!' Toby said with feeling. 'Rotten old St Stinking Stithian's. Wish I could leave.'

'You gotta be sixteen,' said Ginger. 'Shame, innit?'

'What are you going to do then?' said Cat. 'What job?'

'Dunno. Ain't nuffink much about. Not for a bloke with my qualifications.'

'What are your qualifications?'

'Ain't got none. No GCSE's, no nuffink. Could be a brain surgeon, I s'pose, or Prime Minister; else I could sweep the streets like me dad says . . . Let's talk about sunnink else – I 'ate school an' I 'ate exams an' I don't wanna think about jobs.'

Cat had a far-away look in her eyes. 'Exams aren't everything,' she said. 'I failed mine, as a matter of fact.'

'Did you?' said Jess, switching her attention from the little boy, who was trembling on the brink of eruption. 'What exams? "A" levels?'

'Hardly. I'm not supposed to tell you, you know, not really, but I don't suppose it matters now – it was all so long ago . . . I wasn't much good at school, you see. College, it was, strictly speaking; the Academy for Developing Fairies. That's a very dirty laugh, Toby; you should be ashamed of yourself. Don't *grin* so, Jess.'

'Sorry. Where was it – this College?'

'You're not supposed to know that either, but who cares any more? A place called Hy Brazil. It's a floating island – mortals can't see it. They were a frightfully goody-goody lot, those other fairies. Talk about twee! They made me sick. Incy-wincy squeak-squeak.'

'But how did you fail your exams?'

'I've changed my mind. I don't want to tell you. It's rather embarrassing and it all seems childish now.'

'Oh, come *on*, Cat – you can't leave it there!' insisted Jess.

'I'll tell you 'ow I failed mine,' said Ginger. 'I never knew nuffink, that's 'ow. Easy peasy.'

'But I bet you weren't like that, were you, Cat?' said Jess.

'Well, no, actually. I was rather hot stuff. The fact is, I was bored with College. I don't think I ever wanted to be a traditional fairy – too namby-pamby.

I rather fancied being a Wizard, but they wouldn't hear of it, of course; strictly men only in those days. I failed because I insulted the Grand High Sorcerer – the sort of headmaster of the College, a frightful old bore called the Worshipful Master Blaise. I never liked him – he used to creep about in cloth slippers and try to catch you doing something you shouldn't. Ugh! Nasty man. Gave me the shivers.'

'So what did you do?'

'It was all very silly, really. I should have known better. We had a practical exam, you see – in the Alchemy Lab, it was. We were each given a frog and we had to change it into a Prince – you know the type, pretty fellows who fall in love with milkmaids and live happily ever after. Utterly wet, in other words. We had to line up our Princes afterwards to be marked – so much for Elegance, so much for Charm, and Valour and Wit and Handsomeness . . . And Puddingheadedness and Milkmaid-satisfaction, I shouldn't wonder,' she added wickedly. 'They had given me the worst frog, a skinny old thing, a bit greenish and slow, and it reminded me of someone . . . It reminded me so much, in fact, that I just couldn't resist it . . .'

Jess gasped, 'Oh dear! I can see it all! You changed it into the Worshipful Whatsisname, didn't you!'

'Mm . . . the Worshipful Master Blaise, yes . . . It was a superb likeness, if I say it myself. Triffic. But the real one was Not Amused, especially when it argued with him about which *was* the real one. Quite a row that turned out to be, with everyone taking sides and some of the wizards laying bets. What a giggle! They failed me, of course, despite some of the younger warlocks pleading on my behalf – I was quite popular with them, you know.'

'Yeah, I bet you was,' said Ginger. 'I can just imagine. I seen you in action at the Disco the other night.'

'Yes – well – never mind that,' said Cat hastily.

'What did they do with you then?' asked Jess. 'What happens to failed fairies?'

'I was given one more chance. They took away most of my powers and gave me a Provisional Licence and sent me to be nanny to silly old Gurion. And you know what happened to him.'

Jess opened her mouth to ask more, but was interrupted by a loud yell of pure rage, which was followed by a chorus of squeals of mixed delight and terror; the little boy had finally erupted, and was hurling well-rotted seaweed. Several tiny girls began hurling it back; some less spirited ones began to cry, and a number of large red Mums began converging on the centre of the disturbance, like battleships. One tiny child sat apart, thoughtfully eating a starfish.

'You'd better rescue Flora,' said Cat to no one in particular. Jess rolled her eyes heavenwards ('Why is it always *me*!') and struggled into the yowling mob. Flora was busy, piling on more seaweed; it was good fun, and she wanted to stay. Jess had to drag her off by main force.

By the time she had returned and Flora had calmed down Cat was no longer in the mood to tell about her past. She was admiring a driftwood mermaid that Ginger had carved.

'You are clever, Ginge! Isn't she lovely? Look, Jess – did you ever see such a gorgeous little tail? You really are an artist, Ginger. Listen, there's something

I'd like you to do for me; you know that Mr Menon is miniaturising Clara? Well, I shall want a properly designed cabinet to put her in. Could you do that? Design it, I mean. I'm sure Gary would help to make it.'

'Yeah – I'd like that. Gimme time to think it over, though – you want sunnink special for that job ... Yeah ... I've got me own ideas, mind. Can I do what I like?'

They continued to chat together about Clara, and Jess couldn't get another word out of Cat about her past. Jess was cross. It was so frustrating! There were still too many mysteries about Cat and she needed some answers. Could you believe *anything* of what she said? What was she doing here, truly? How long would she stay? If she disappeared as suddenly as she had arrived, what would become of them then? Why didn't Toby – or Ginger, come to that – ever seem to worry about these things?

'Why is it always left to me?' she muttered angrily to herself. She got up to go to visit the rockpools; she glanced back as she strode away, trying to think of something cutting to say that would make her mood felt. 'I think that mermaid's *rude!*' she shouted, with a toss of her head.

Cat wanted to go shopping in the nearby town. 'Do you want to come with me, Jess? I'm going to buy presents for Gary and Hyacinth and Toni and Mr Menon.'

'I'd better,' said Jess. 'Anyway, I'd like to buy them presents, too.'

Jess had come to see it as her duty to look after Cat when shopping, in case she made trouble – with banks and little green men, for example. On this trip, it was the automatic doors of a supermarket. Jess hadn't thought of that. Cat was fascinated, of course, and wanted to play with them for ages. By the time Jess dragged her away the damage was done; the doors stood wide open until a customer approached – and then they closed. They could not be forced open, although plenty of people tried. When the victims turned away in disgust the doors opened; whereupon the people gladly rushed forward – and the doors closed again. This process repeated itself indefinitely. Cat laughed until she cried.

'I think,' said Jess firmly, 'that we'd better go back to the beach. You're not safe to be let out, Cat.'

'But I'm having such fun!'

'We'll get locked up. Come along *at once*!'

Cat made a face and put her tongue out.

Half-way back to the hotel, Jess said, 'Stop the car, please. I want to talk to you.'

'Oh, dear,' said Cat. 'Are you going to tick me off for being naughty?'

'Cat, will you promise to tell me the truth?'

'No, I shouldn't think so,' said Cat promptly. 'It might not be good for you.'

Jess was a bit taken aback by this, but at least it was honest.

'Well, are you really a fairy?'

'Could be. Sort of. I told you that right at the beginning, didn't I?'

'But – can you really do magic?'

'You're getting awfully forceful, Jess, not nearly so shy as you used to be. I'm pleased. And you have an enquiring mind, haven't you! Why aren't you top of the class? Your school reports aren't too wonderful.'

'Oh, I hate school. Mouldy old St Stink's. And I don't like Miss Pindlebury, our teacher, and old Cussy Custard the Headmaster's a right brain cell, and the boys are too rough, and – hey! You're changing the subject. We're talking about *you*, not me.'

'Well, I am here to do good. That's about the long and the short of it.'

'But how did you *get* here? Where are you *from*?'

'I've told you – Muckle Eigg. And as for how I got here, what would *you* do if they shut you up in a boring rock for years and years?'

'I'd try to escape.'

'Well, then.'

'But *how*?'

'Ah, that'd be telling. It's time we were moving – we're wasting the low tide. I thought you wanted to look for a sea-mouse?'

And that was that. Jess never really got much closer to the truth. Talking to Cat was like trying to divide water, or as Ginger put it, 'like fightin' with marshmallows'.

The hotel provided many activities, like the swimming races which Toby entered (but came nowhere) and the Punch and Judy show which Flora demanded to see every afternoon although it never varied and she knew every tiny detail of it by heart. Uncle Oz evidently enjoyed the meals and the whisky and ignored everything else, though his friendship with Dr Haddock flourished and made a big difference to him, especially when the good Doctor took to joining him in the bar in the evenings to discuss winkles. Aunt Spot watched television, but even she was infected by the holiday spirit – she found several like-minded old ladies who gathered in the Sun Lounge after lunch to snooze and knit and gossip about their favourite news-readers and the scandalous goings-on in 'East Enders' and such like important matters. Aunt Spot, in fact, had a tremendous personal triumph when the hotel staff put on a TV quiz for the Old Folk and she won by an enormous lead. They gave her a little tin fish on a stand for a prize and she was so proud of it that you would have thought it was solid gold. She took it everywhere with her.

'I've got a job for you, Toby,' said Cat one night at dinner, when they had been talking about Aunt Spot and the Mighty Fish. 'When we get home we'll buy a video machine for her – you can show her how it works and take her round to the Video Hire shop on the High Street. She'll love that, and it'll get her out of the house from time to time. It'll do her good.'

'OK,' said Toby, 'but what about us? Do we get a video too?'

'Mm, I should think so. Why not? Good fun. It'll do *you* good!'

Jess didn't like this talk of things to be done 'when we get home'. It seemed to shorten the holiday. She wanted to enjoy every minute of it and not look ahead. On the other hand she thought a lot about Toni and Hyacinth and Gary; she missed them. Often, alone in bed at night, she thought particularly of Hyacinth, who was so warm and loving and safe. Much as she loved Cat, Cat was – well, *dangerous*. That seemed to be the best description. You couldn't feel really secure with her, as you could with Hyacinth – you never knew what she might do next.

'If Cat is *really* a fairy godmother,' thought Jess,

'I'd like to have Hyacinth as a sort of real mother. At least she's practical – she knows how things ought to be done, which is more than you can say about Cat. And I'd have Ginger as a sort of older brother, and Toni and Gary as Uncles.'

She sighed to herself. 'If only life were that simple!' It was a nice idea, safe and comfortable, and she thought about it a lot, especially as she had an uneasy feeling deep down that Cat might not stay for ever. She had, after all, appeared suddenly and unexpectedly; it was quite possible, thought Jess, that she might go out one day and not come back. You never really got any warning with Cat.

'She's *just not reliable*,' thought Jess.

'Aunt Spot,' announced Toby importantly, 'has gone right off her trolley. I always knew she would.'

Jess, Cat and Ginger looked up from their puddings and exchanged grins across the dinner table.

'She has!' insisted Toby. 'I've been watching her. She comes creeping out of her room in the afternoons – once she's had her Little Nap, that is – and she totters off to the sun lounge with two more old biddies.'

'So what?' said Jess. 'I think it's nice that she's made friends. I expect they talk about television.'

'They don't!' said Toby scornfully. 'I'll tell you what they do. They gamble!'

'Gerroff!' said Ginger. 'What do you mean? Work the old fruit machines, do they?'

'No – course not. They play cards, that's what they do. I've seen 'em, through the window from the outside. They've caught an old man, too, and he plays with them, and they have all this money stacked up on the table in front of them.'

'They can't have *caught* an old man,' said Jess. 'They couldn't *make* him play.'

'They have, too! Like Flora and her mob caught that little boy and buried him in stinking seaweed. He didn't like it, and this old man doesn't, either. You should see him – he looks as cheerful as school dinners. He sits there scowling and poking at his cards, and Aunt Spot kicks him under the table!'

Cat giggled. 'You do see the worst in things, Toby. They're only playing bridge, and it's hardly gambling – only ten points for a penny. It's all quite innocent, you know. Well, nearly innocent – Aunt Spot cheats, actually; that's what the little kicks are all about. They're signals. She and her partner have only won about eight pence so far. He's called Mr Baggs, by the way, and he's a retired Station Master. He's rather sweet. If you like railway men, that is.'

'And Aunt Spot *does* like them,' exclaimed Jess. 'Is that it?'

'Mmm,' nodded Cat.

Jess giggled. 'Is it true? Really? Oh, honestly, Cat, it's all your fault. Who'd have thought it! It's this holiday of yours – you fixed it up, and it's doing us *all* good. There's Flora running around like a savage, jabbering non-stop and terrifying little boys, and Toby going native in the surf and showing off to all the girls—'

'I do not!'

'Yes, you do – I've seen you! We've all seen you. You love it. And Ginger being all artistic, carving naughty mermaids and one thing and another . . . And Uncle Oz hurtling about all day with Dr Haddock, chasing winkles, poor things, and now you tell me there's Aunt Spot madly in love with retired railway men and cheating at cards. When I think back to what we were all like before you came ... Well, we wouldn't have done all this six weeks ago, I can tell you!'

'And what about you?' said Cat wistfully. 'Have I done you any good?'

'Oh, yes, of course you have! Lots and lots of good. I'm – well, I'm just happy!'

And Cat smiled and smiled as if Jess had pressed a switch and lit her up like a lamp; or someone had given her a present of her heart's desire.

In the remaining days Cat became browner, Flora's hair bleached almost white, Ginger won first prize in a sand-sculpting competition, Uncle Oz accompanied Dr Haddock all day in hot pursuit of winkles, Toby gained such expertise on the surfboard that he was the envy of all the other kids on the beach, and Jess caught an octopus.

It was a tiny octopus, not much bigger than a walnut, but it had eight arms with suckers and squirted ink in the proper manner, it jet-propelled itself backwards, it changed from transparent to a deep plum purple when angry, and Jess marvelled at it for its jewel-like perfection. She kept it for most of a day, carefully refreshing the water in its bucket frequently so that it didn't get too hot. The octopus made the holiday complete for Jess. It was the crowning glory of the happy, sunny days.

She gazed at it in fascination, half-unbelieving. To her, an octopus was something you only met in storybooks, a mythical beast, strange and wonderful;

and yet here it was, alive and pulsing, turning its eight limbs into an umbrella shape or drawing them together like the segments of an orange, a magic thing alive and real in a rockpool on an English beach. It was almost, thought Jess, like a wish come true. No one really believed that wishes could come true; in stories everything comes out right in the end, and they-all-lived-happily-ever-after, but Jess knew that real life wasn't like that. Yet the octopus was here, something from a fable, here in the real world, making a link between what might be and what is.

Jess marvelled at it. It made her feel that life isn't always predictable, that magical things *do* happen. After all, if you can stumble upon an octopus, of all things, *anything* might be possible.

Cat has the right attitude, thought Jess, rising to her feet. She let the little creature go, with her blessing, and then stood with her legs apart, like Cat.

'Anything is possible,' she whispered. She thrust out her chin, like Cat. 'I can do anything,' she said, as if trying it on for size. It felt good.

'I *can* do anything!' she said firmly.

She raised her arms and shouted to the empty sky, 'I CAN DO ANYTHING!'

Then she smiled a little secret smile, like Cat.

9

A New Home

The time came to go home. It always does. Other families trooped out in orderly fashion to their cars, luggage neatly stowed away, children seated in the back, mother and father tidily strapped in the front seats. Not so the Murgatroyds. Cat made an awful muddle of the packing, to start with, until Jess – the new, super-confident, I-can-do-anything Jess – took over.

'Nearly all the clothes are dirty,' she said. There's no point in trying to pack them carefully, and besides, we want room in the cases for all our sea shells and presents and precious things. I shall just shove everything else into bin bags.'

And she did. She told Cat to go and look after Toby and Flora while she, Jess, collected everything together, packed it, and got Ginger to load it into the cars.

By then, Cat had lost Flora. 'I only turned my back for a moment,' she wailed. 'I just wanted a last browse in the bookshop.'

'Oooh, you're hopeless!' scolded Jess. 'I can't trust you to do anything, can I? Leave it to me – I'll find her.'

After a lot of hard searching, Flora was found in the Hot Pool. She and the Tiny Mob were ganging up on the seaweed boy again, apparently trying to drown him a sip at a time. He clearly didn't like it and was fast approaching boiling point. Flora didn't want to leave the fun, and it took quite a lot of time and effort to fish her out, squealing and dripping, and then Jess had to chase her about in the sunshine to dry her off, because all the towels were packed.

Meanwhile, they discovered later, Uncle Oz went to bring his car to the hotel main door in order to load his and Aunt Spot's luggage. Colonel Armstrong-Siddeley, however, wasn't having it; he refused to start.

'Can't go on parade in this state, man. Need a jolly good bout of spit-and-polish. Nice wash down and a bit of a buff.'

So poor old Oz, scarlet with fury, had to go to the hotel kitchen to beg a bucket and hot water, detergent and soft cloths, and spent the next hour scrubbing and sluicing while the Colonel nagged at him. And while all that was going on, Aunt Spot drifted off to find her cronies for a last cheating-session at cards, so that even when he had finished Uncle Oz couldn't leave but had to wait for the game to end.

By then it was lunch-time and Aunt Spot decided that they might as well stay for the meal at the hotel, and have a little nap in the Sun Lounge after it; in fact, there were so many delays of one kind or another – Dr Haddock arrived with a particularly interesting winkle, for instance, and Aunt Spot spent twenty minutes looking for her glasses, which she was wearing at the time – that it was late afternoon before they eventually set off, and Cat and the others were already home.

*

'Have you *seen* the bathroom!' yelled Jess at the top of her voice. 'It's fantastic! There are carpets on the floor and beautiful tiles on the walls and a new loo and everything! The bath is plum coloured!'

Nobody was listening. Toby and Ginger were checking the Rumpus Room to make sure that the workmen had not spoiled it, Cat was gloating over the new carpets and wallpaper everywhere, and Flora had taken her rats to see Toni.

Cat came further up the stairs, lovingly stroking the varnished banister rail. 'Let's have a look at your bedroom, Jess.'

Jess hadn't even thought of it; her bedroom was a cold, dark little box, with plain cream walls and worn green linoleum on the floor. Her dresses hung on a rail at one side, covered with plastic bags, and her other clothes were stored in a plain chest of drawers – and that was it. There wasn't even a chair to sit on. Jess had never used the room except as a place to sleep.

'Come on,' said Cat excitedly. 'I do hope you like it. I'm sure you will. It's a surprise! You will like it, won't you – please?'

Jess liked the door, which had become an interesting smoky blue colour instead of dirty, chipped cream. She opened it.

'Oh!' she gasped, and drew breath, and couldn't speak.

Her first impression was of light and colour and flowers, for Hyacinth had arranged a huge bunch like a whole cottage garden in front of the window. They scented the room. Then Jess began to notice the details – the fitted carpet; the bookshelves, beautifully made by Gary; built-in cupboards and wardrobe; the bed-side lamps – the new bed! – a cosy chair; the wallpaper; the central heating radiators . . .

'I haven't done anything about pictures,' said Cat, 'because you ought to choose ones to suit your own taste – or paint them yourself. And you must arrange the things the way you want them – put your books on the shelves, and so on. You do like it, don't you?' she added anxiously.

'It's wonderful,' whispered Jess. 'My own room . . . my very own! Oh, Cat – it's beautiful!'

The door crashed open and Toby came in like a whirlwind. 'Have you seen the bathroom?' he shouted, waving his arms. 'There are plants everywhere! It's like a tropical rainforest! I wouldn't be surprised to find tree-frogs in there! And the hot water's *hot*!'

Mr Menon arrived, looking rather glum.

'What's the matter?' said Cat. 'Are you in trouble?'

'He sure is,' said Gary. 'They gave him the sack. I said they would. Spent too much time here!'

'Oo-er!' said Toby.

'Blimey!' said Ginger. 'That's rotten luck. You'll 'ave to join me, down the old dole queue.'

'It is true, I am afraid,' said Mr Menon, sounding ashamed. 'I do have two months' notice, but after that I shall have to find another job. I am sorry to say that I brought it upon myself.'

Cat smiled at him. 'Don't worry. You have a nice fat fee coming to you for all the hours you have put in on Clara – and I won't embarrass you by asking how many hours you have spent; Clara will tell me – and that'll help to tide you over. After that, we shall see. I have a feeling you won't be out of work for long.'

'Yeah, cheer up,' said Ginger. 'When I leave school I won't 'ave no job neither, an' a fat chance of gettin' one. We'll meet down the Social Security an' 'ave a bit of a natter. Now, come an' show me what you done with old Clara – I gotta put me thinkin' cap on, en'I – make 'er a box or sunnink.'

Jess waited until Mr Menon and Ginger had left before turning to Cat. 'What did you mean, you have an idea he won't be out of work for long?'

Cat smiled vaguely. 'Oh, well. Mr Menon is a very good man with machinery, you know; the best. I'm sure he'll find an excellent job in no time.'

And Jess had to be content with that, although she knew from the way Cat smiled that she was plotting something, and also that Cat was, as usual, avoiding giving a straight answer.

'Look here, Murgatroyd,' said the Colonel one morning after they had been home for a few days, 'been thinkin'. Got an idea for you. You awake? Got your dim little brain in gear?'

'Yes, sir,' said Uncle Oz meekly.

'Right. Well, here it is, then; you should retire.'

'Wha'? Wha' you mean, retire?'

'Plain enough, isn't it? Simple English. Any baboon could grasp that. Retire, you damn fool. Stop work.'

'But – but – I can't! M'factory! It's – it's me livelihood!'

'Nonsense, man. Utter piffle. You don't need a livelihood. You're absolutely filthy rich as it is – got more money than you could jump over. I know that.

107

You know that. Any gibbering orang-utan knows that.'

'But I can't possibly . . . I mean, give up all my . . . me *factory*!' Uncle Oz practically sobbed.

'Course you can. Nothin' to it. Oh, well, take your time,' said the Colonel quite mildly. 'No use rushin' your fences. Not too sharp, are you? Have a little think about it – it'll sink in eventually. We'll get it all cut and dried in a day or two.'

Ginger asked Cat to disappear for a while. 'I'm 'aving sunnink delivered, like, an' it's a secret, an' I don't want you around. An' keep out of your sitting-room for a bit an' all, will you, please?'

Cat was quite happy to go out shopping with Jess. Flora stayed in the kitchen with Hyacinth, making pastry rats with currants for eyes, and Toby went out scrounging.

The little green man was merrily turning cartwheels while the beep-beep mechanism played a cheerful country dance. The policeman had gone and hidden himself, and the traffic was more snarled up than ever. Cat had to be dragged away.

They entered a large department store. 'We must get you some new school uniform,' said Cat cheerily. 'Term starts soon, you know.'

Jess knew perfectly well. She had been feeling happy, but now her heart zoomed down into her boots at the thought of it. She felt slightly sick.

'You're not so thin as you were,' said Cat, busy with a tape-measure. 'You're coming along nicely. We shall make a beauty of you yet.'

Cat turned to the rails of school blazers and coats. 'Oh, this *is* smart,' she said, holding up a neat grey blazer with red braid around the lapels. 'And look – here's the tunic that goes with it. Very posh. It has a red sash to go round it. This is winter uniform, of course. Seems funny to be choosing it in this weather, doesn't it?'

Jess couldn't bear to comment.

'And this'll be the winter coat,' went on Cat regardless. 'I say, this'll be warm. And *so* well made – just look at the lining. Expensive, mind you, but well worth it. You'd look a million dollars in this.'

'Wrong colour,' said Jess miserably. 'St Stink's is a sort of dirty green. Toby says it's like puke.'

'Tut-tut, rude boy,' said Cat, not paying attention. 'Look at this – isn't it sweet?' It was a red wrap-around skirt with many pleats, very brief. 'You wear it for netball, I think. It's gorgeous . . . I wonder if they've got one in my size? It'd make a smashing mini-skirt – with black tights, I think – for discos . . .'

'You couldn't possibly,' sniffed Jess. 'It'd be indecent.'

'Yes, it would, wouldn't it,' said Cat wickedly. 'I *must* have one!'

'Look, why are we bothering with all this?' Jess wanted to know. 'It's none of it anything *like* St Stinking Stithian's, I tell you. Dreadful rotten place.' She felt very close to tears.

'Oh,' said Cat, opening her eyes wide. 'Didn't you realise? Haven't you caught on yet? You're not going back *there* – not ever again!'

When they returned home, laden with bags and parcels and boxes, they were greeted by Toby in the entrance hall, bouncing about and yelling.

'Come and see what we've done! Ginger and Winston and me – we've had a fabulous time. You'll be ever so surprised, honest. Come and see – come and see! It's Ginger's idea really, but I helped.'

Ginger appeared from upstairs. 'Yeah, Cat, come an' look. I 'ope you like it.'

Mr Menon stood smiling behind him.

The parcels were dumped and everyone dashed up to Cat's apartment.

'Da-da!' sang Ginger, flinging open the door. 'There y'are. Whadda yer think?'

Jess and Cat looked around, puzzled. Toby and Ginger stood grinning. There was no sign of Clara, and the only thing they could see that was different was a large, comfy-looking arm-chair with pretty floral upholstery, which stood beside the fireplace, opposite the television set.

Ginger laughed loudly, wrinkling up his freckled face. 'You don't get it, do ya!' Mr Menon's smile grew wider.

'No, I don't,' said Cat, thoroughly puzzled. 'It's a very nice chair, and of course it's a surprise because I didn't know it was coming, but I didn't expect you to be installing new furniture – I thought you were making a box for Clara.'

'That's it, that's it, that's *it*!' yelled Toby.

'What – the *chair*?' said Cat incredulously.

''Sright. Good, ennit? Triffic! 'Ere, you come an' sit down. Come on, darlin' – take the weight off yer feet.'

Gingerly, looking as if she thought the chair might bite, Cat sat down.

'Hello, dear,' said a friendly, familiar voice. 'How nice that we can be so close. Lean back and relax.'

In fact, Cat shot up as if she had been stung. 'Good grief! What on earth have you done?'

'Mr Menon 'elped,' said Ginger. ''E come round and done the wiring, like. We got all Clara's innards inside the arms – in here, look, you can see where Hyacinth stitched it up again after – an' we put the little speakers from the voice wossname inside the 'eadrest. So you can sit down with yer feet up an' 'ave a nice little chat with Clara any time yer like.'

'Amazing!' said Cat. 'A computer you can sit in! You're a genius, you know, Ginger. Who ever would have thought of anything like it?'

Mr Menon began to clap, and the others joined in.

''Ere, leave it out!' said Ginger. 'You'll make me go all shy!'

'Impossible!' shouted Toby, and they all laughed.

The next morning, an extraordinary thing happened. Two letters arrived, one for Uncle Oz and one for Aunt Spot. The extraordinary thing about this was that they *never* had any letters, either of them, ever. They had no friends, of course, at least not until now. Uncle Oz's letter was from Dr Haddock, telling him all about a rare winkle he had just discovered – 'a delightful creature, my dear chap, most unusual. There appears to be quite a little colony of them in the Laminaria zone at extreme low water. I do wish you could be here to see it.'

Aunt Spot's letter was from the retired Station Master, who was a permanent resident at the hotel where they had stayed (he had won a big Premium Bond prize which enabled him to afford it). It was a long, rambling letter which didn't really get any-where, because the old boy's memory was somewhat adrift, and he tended to forget what he had just written and start all over again. What it boiled down to was that he felt lonely now that he hadn't got Aunt Spot to cheat at cards with and he wished she was there. He called her 'my dear Matilda' several times in the letter (and 'my dear Miriam' once), which sent her all of a dither.

Anyway, when Uncle Oz set off for work he was thinking about Cornwall, and happy strolls along the sea-shore with his friend Haddock. He actually began to smile to himself.

'I say, Murgatroyd,' the Colonel interrupted his pleasant daydreams. 'This retirement business. End of the week suit you?'

'Wha'? Oh, crikey!'

'Don't tell me you haven't thought about it. Told you to, didn't I? We shan't be drivin' down *this* road after Friday next, and that's flat. Thought what you're goin' to do with yourself, have you?'

At this point Uncle Oz suffered a very strange sensation; he goggled and gasped and spluttered; he had had an idea!

'G'd Lor'! I say – just thoughta-sumthin'! Lumme!'

'Come on, come on – spit it out, man. Don't shilly-shally. Brief and to the point, now.'

Uncle Oz gulped. 'Cornwall,' he gasped. 'Wouldn't mind – you know – going back to see old Haddock . . .' His voice trailed away as the glory of the Idea really sank in.

'Splendid, splendid,' applauded the Colonel. 'Buy a little place down there, will you? Manor House or somethin'? Like it down there, y'know. Bracin', very. Good for me carburettors. Righty-ho, old lad – orf we go down the jolly old motorway; on Saturday. Glad that's fixed.'

Meanwhile, Aunt Spot was writing, in her thin spidery script with a lot of underlining, a long letter to 'my *dear* Claude' at the hotel. A lot of it was very boring, describing her tapestry work and her knitting and her favourite TV personalities, but no doubt her dear Claude loved it, especially since he would forget most of it at once. The really important part was where she admitted that she missed him, and all their *happy hours* together playing dishonest games of cards, and that she would *very much* like to *return* to Cornwall *soon*, and hoped to *stay* for a *nice long time*, if only she could get her brother ('dearest Oswald') to *agree*.

'Clara,' said Cat, leaning back on Clara's ample cushions and wiggling her bare toes to make the nail varnish dry, 'I have just found out that Uncle Oz wishes to retire to Cornwall, pretty well at once. Do you like this colour, by the way?'

'It's a *bit* pink,' said Clara judiciously. 'Something with a touch of silver in it might look more sophisticated. Yes, I know about Oz, of course. The Colonel and I fixed it up between us. It's all arranged. Did you know Aunt Spot is going with him?'

'I hoped that she might. Did you fix that too?'

'Yes, dear. It was more difficult, but I had an idea which worked in the end.'

'Oh? And what was that?'

'Claude Baggs, dear. You told me about him, remember? I have managed to establish an electronic link with the television set in his room at the hotel. I have been flashing Aunt Spot's name on the screen for a few micro-seconds every minute. Even though he's so forgetful it still penetrated eventually, so he has been thinking about her all the time. He wrote her a letter, and she wrote to him, and she is going down there with Uncle Oz on Saturday. Triffic, isn't it?'

'Triffic, indeed!' said Cat. 'You've been talking to Ginger, haven't you. How do you know about the letters?'

'Hyacinth told me. She got roped in to help Aunt Spot pack, so she had heard all about it, several times, poor dear.'

'And is Aunt Spot pleased?'

'Oh, I should say so, dear! She's frightfully excited – just can't wait to go. Sweet, really. She's gone all girlish.'

'That's wonderful,' sighed Cat. 'My plans are all beginning to come together. You are clever, Clara.'

'No, no, dear – you are the clever one. You made me, remember!'

The next day was very busy. Aunt Spot drove everyone nearly demented with her packing, so that Uncle Oz, who had decided not to go to work so that *he* could pack, went to work anyway and made his workers lives a misery all day.

Cat took the children out, mainly to buy new school uniform for Toby.

'Isn't it wonderful,' carolled Jess, dancing along the pavement, 'no more Stinky Stithian's – lovely, lovely, lovely St Catherine's instead!'

'They've got a whole roomful of computers there,

you know,' said Toby with relish. 'Old Cussy Custard wouldn't even have *one*! "We are not here to play with toys, children,"' he said, mimicking Cussy's soppy voice, '"We are here to *learn*." Loony old brain cell,' he added scornfully.

'Hurray for St Catherine's,' sang Jess. 'I can't wait for term to start.'

'We should call it St Cat's,' said Toby.

So of course, nobody ever called it anything else.

Cat called a meeting in the kitchen at coffee time. Flora was busy moulding little green men out of pastry coloured with food-dye, with Hyacinth's help, and Hyacinth had to pretend to be the workmen coming to 'mend' them.

Cat said, 'Listen, everybody. I have something important to tell you. It is a question of doing good.'

Toby, Jess and Ginger cheered ironically, and wondered what mischief she was up to now.

'This little green man rolls up,' stated Flora.

'As you know,' continued Cat, 'Uncle Oz and Aunt Spot are off to Cornwall tomorrow.'

More cheers. 'Good riddance to bad rubbish!' shouted Toby.

'Whoops! He rolled away. Naughty little green man.'

'Poor old Cornwall,' giggled Jess. 'I say, Ginger, do you like my St Cat's hat? Triffic, isn't it?'

'Shut up,' said Cat. 'I am trying to do good here, but if you don't put a sock in it and pay attention I shall turn you into a stick insect.'

'*Naughty* little green man! Smack, smack.'

'That's not fair!' said Jess. 'I'm not that thin any more, you said so yourself.'

'Yes you are,' said Toby. 'You're a skinny Lizzie Jess pest, and that hat looks like a tea cosy.'·

'It does not! It's a lovely hat! It's traditional, that's what it is. It's—'

'Quiet!' commanded Cat. 'That's enough. We have good things to discuss. Are you all listening? Now, Uncle Oz is going to retire. The question is, when he has gone who will manage the washing machine factory?'

Nobody said anything (except Flora: 'This little green man gone all flat – look! Aaaaah! Hyacinth mend him!').

'Well, I'll tell you who. Mr Menon!'

Everyone turned to stare at Mr Menon, who spluttered into his coffee. 'But – but – my dear Cat – I couldn't! I don't know about washing machines, or about managing factories!'

'Hogwash!' said Cat firmly. 'You have too low an opinion of yourself. You are capable of doing anything you set your mind to. You, Mr Menon, are very clever. You could organise that place standing on your head.'

'Poor little green man. All flat.'

Mr Menon sat with his mouth open.

'I dunno,' said Ginger. 'You're a rum 'un, you are – you're out of work, ain't cha? Got no job. I'd 'ave thought this was an offer yer can't refuse. Anyroad, you'd do the job smashin'. I know yer would.'

'Ginger is right,' said Cat. 'You are the ideal man for the position. Anyway, it's all fixed up. The Colonel has told Uncle Oz – and has made him agree, of course – and Clara has told the wages computer at the factory. You'll get a jolly good salary, by the way, and a car that goes with the job. You will be a very important chap – Managing Director!'

'Oh my goodness! What an idea!'

'Little green man goes plop plop plop.'

'No, darlin', not in Hyacinth's nice coffee.'

'There'll be a lot to do,' went on Cat. 'Things are in an awful pickle there. Fortunately, Uncle Oz is now so rich that there won't be any trouble with the expense. You'll be able to do whatever is needed to put the factory into good shape. You'll be able to do a lot of good, if you think about it.'

'He likes it in the coffee – nice and warm. Swim-swim, swim-swim, little green man.'

'I'll tell you sunnink,' said Ginger, who had been thinking. 'Them washing machines is rotten. They're wossname, you know, famous for it – notorious. You oughta do sunnink about that.'

'Well, of course,' said Mr Menon thoughtfully, 'there is no reason why they should be so bad. It's a question of design really.'

'He goes splish splash – look, Hyacinth.'

'They're rotten because Uncle Oz thought he'd sell more if they were cheap,' said Toby, rolling his eyes. 'But he didn't, silly old brain cell, because no one was daft enough to buy one twice.'

'Oh – he's gone all sticky. Oh dear!'

'Tell you what,' said Ginger, 'if you made really triffic machines, that worked proper and never broke down, I bet they'd sell like 'ot cakes. An' another thing – they *look* rotten. They look cheap an' nasty, them Murgatroyds. All flimsy, an' the paint chips off, an' they're too narrow. They go rusty in the shop, let alone when anyone puts water in 'em. No one would buy one if they wasn't desperate.'

'What would *you* do, Ginger, to improve them? If you had a free hand?' said Cat, chin on her fists.

'Let Hyacinth wipe little handies, darlin'. Come on, now.'

'Cor, I wouldn't 'alf sharpen 'em up! I'd make 'em look friendly, like, for starters, an' do all the controls different – so as the knobs didn't fall off, for one thing – an' I'd 'ave 'em all nice colours, an' they wouldn't be called Murgatroyds no more, 'cos that's a bad name *if* yer like! We'd call 'em Menons – yeah, that's it, the Menon Magnificent for the perfect wash! I'll design you a nice little thingummy, logo, to go on the front, like – an' – an' – hey! Yeah! Triffic! I just 'ad a great idea – I'd 'ave a voice wossname in 'em, that said, like, "Please clean my filter," or "I'm ready now, empty me".'

'Wonderful,' said Cat, applauding.

'*This* little green man's a *good* little green man. He goes bleep bleep bleep.'

Toby laughed. 'Great! And it could say "Stop stuffing me, I'm full," and "Don't you dare come near me with those smelly socks".'

'Or "Please put Toby in me – he's a mucky little boy!"' yelled Jess.

'Mr Menon,' said Cat, smiling broadly, 'allow me to present my very clever and talented friend Ginger. He is your new Chief Designer.'

''Ere! You don't mean it, do you? Me? A job?'

'I most certainly do mean it. People with your artistic ability and original ideas are very rare and worth their weight in gold. It'll be a proper job, with a good salary and a posh car – when you're old enough to drive it. I suggest that Mr Menon should re-design the works of the machines, but you will make suggestions – like the one about the voice wossname – and you will decide what they look like. You will work together, in fact. Do you approve, Mr Menon?'

'Oh, yes! Yes, please! A truly splendid idea,' said Mr Menon. 'What a team we will make!'

'Cor! Triffic!' breathed Ginger.

The next day, Saturday, everyone turned out to wave goodbye to Uncle Oz and Aunt Spot. The Colonel, gleaming and splendid, was loaded with mounds of luggage, including Aunt Spot's television and video recorder and a crate of whisky from the locked cupboard in the dining-room. He had a private word with Clara by radio link before they left, promising to keep in touch every day so that Cat knew what was going on and any of her instructions could be passed on to him.

Aunt Spot and Uncle Oz were as excited as two kids. The truth of the matter was that they had never had any fun, not for years and years and years, until Cat had forced them to go on holiday, and now that they had had a taste of it they couldn't wait for more. Uncle Oz was purple in the face with pleasure and anticipation, and Aunt Spot dithered around dropping things and losing things and generally behaving like a two year old.

At last, the Colonel purred smoothly away from the kerb.

'Goodbye! Goodbye! Have a happy retirement. Give our love to Cornwall. Drive carefully.'

'I'm almost sorry to see them go,' said Jess.

'Almost,' said Toby.

'They'll be very happy in Cornwall,' said Cat.

'They won't be coming back here. You can always go and visit them, you know, if you want to. It would be nice to have another holiday, wouldn't it? And besides,' she added, 'I suspect you may have to go down there for a wedding before long.'

'Wedding? What wedding?'

'Come *on*, Jess! Don't be slow. Of course, dear old Claude Baggs will have to remember to ask her . . . Maybe I can get Clara to drop him a hint.'

'You don't mean Aunt Spot, do you?'

'Certainly dear! Do wake up. Why else do you think she's so excited?'

Jess was lost for words.

The rest of the morning was spent in work of one kind or another. There were name-tapes to be sewn on the new school clothes, which Cat made a muddle of until Hyacinth took them away from her. Flora had a lot of work to do – snails to be stroked and counted, and a pramful of little green men to take for a walk. Jess went out with her for a bit.

Gary and Ginger, with Toby to get in the way, gave Aunt Spot's rooms a thorough spring-cleaning, even if it was the end of summer.

'Gary and Hyacinth are moving in,' explained Cat. 'Aunt Spot's rooms are so much nicer than their council flat and of course they won't have to pay rent. It will do them good. Besides,' she added slyly, 'they're needed here.'

The gang came round with all Gary and Hyacinth's things on the garbage truck and helped to move it in. Hyacinth was so happy that she sang all the time. The gang stayed to lunch and drank a lot of Toni's red Italian wine and nobody's bins were emptied that afternoon.

10

Night Magic

At bedtime, after she had looked in on Flora and made sure that Toby had actually had a bath and had actually washed himself in it, Cat came into Jess's room to say good-night and have a cuddle, as she usually did. She put her arms around Jess, snuggled up and gave a great sigh of satisfaction.

'All my plans have worked out,' she said happily. 'You know, Jess, it's a grand feeling, doing good.'

'Mm,' said Jess sleepily. 'Won't it be super without Aunt Spot and Uncle Oz.'

'It will indeed. You'll be able to relax and enjoy yourselves. School starts soon – looking forward to it?'

'Yes – I am, as a matter of fact. I shall make friends at St Cat's, I'm sure.'

'Of course you will. They're nice kids, there. And you can bring them home to play and have Toni's cream teas. Hyacinth can't *wait*. She wants the whole house full of children, she says. I *do* like my red mini-skirt – doesn't it look nice?'

'It's indecent. I told you it would be.'

'Yes, but I've got such good legs, haven't I!'

Jess giggled, and Cat grinned at her. 'You happy, Jess?'

'Oh, yes, Cat, ever so! I haven't been so happy since – well, you know.'

'Yes, dear, I know . . . You really did need a fairy godmother, didn't you.'

'Mm, yes. It's been a wonderful summer. The best ever. Think of all the fun we've had! And all the friends we've made . . . The holiday in Cornwall, and doing up the Rumpus Room – and look at my gorgeous bedroom!'

'You like it, don't you?'

'Yes,' said Jess dreamily. 'It's my own special place with my own special things in it and I love it.'

'Have I done you good? Truly?'

'Of course you have! You know you have. I used to be so shy and unhappy, you have no idea. I was afraid of almost everything – especially school, and Aunt Spot and Uncle Oz, and going out and meeting people. But you've changed all that. Now I feel that I can do anything! It's all due to you, Cat.'

'I am so pleased. You are twice the girl you were. And I don't want to be immodest—'

'Hoo! Never!' said Jess.

'—but I think I've done good to the others as well.'

'You have done us *all* good, Cat – Toby and Flora and me, and Ginger and Mr Menon and Gary and Hyacinth and Toni . . . And the tourists and the men who repair the traffic lights. *And* all the people who work at the factory. You're wonderful, Cat.' Jess yawned hugely. 'I forgot Aunt Spot and Uncle Oz – and Dr Haddock, I suppose, and poor old lonely Mr Baggs.'

'It's not too bad a record, if you say it like that,' said Cat, 'for a failed fairy. Things *are* different now. I said they would be.'

'So you did,' murmured Jess, as Cat kissed her eyelids and she slid away, ever so gently, into sleep.

*

That night Jess had a dream.

She dreamed that Cat came into her room and did magic. Cat wore a filmy nightgown that seemed to glow with soft, subtle light and there was stardust in her hair. She sat on the bed beside Jess and was still for a long time, or so Jess dreamed it. Jess could smell her fragrance and felt her cool hands on her brow. Cat whispered, 'This is special magic, Jess,' as her finger tips stroked her hair. 'Can you feel it?' Jess *could* feel it as the fingers smoothed away the anxious lines on her forehead and relaxed her eyelids. 'It is to make you strong. You can do anything, you know, Jess, if you set your mind to it. You can be anyone you want to be, but especially you can be *yourself*. There is no need to be afraid. Come. I will show you something.'

The bed was a dream bed, deep and soft and white like the clouds. It floated, easily, silently, smoothly, high above the city, whose lights sparkled like cold fire.

'Do you see the city?' murmured Cat, stroking softly. 'It is your city. It is where you live.'

The bed rose higher and higher, but with no sense of movement.

'Do you see the land?' said Cat quietly.

The whole country lay spread out below them like a map, a dark shape sprinkled with fairy-dust cities, floating in the dark, featureless sea. 'It is your land, Jess, yours for your lifetime,' said Cat as the shape swung by, slowly, with the turning world.

Higher still, and there was the whole planet itself, half in darkness and still asleep, half ablaze with the light of the new day. The dream took them smoothly around, passing over many lands to the bright side.

'Look!' breathed Cat. Dreaming, Jess saw the blue world with its white banks of cloud and icy poles magnificent against the black starlit curtain of space.

'It's – beautiful!'

'It is a wonderful world, Jess, complicated and magical. It is your world, dearest child – you are ready to find your place in it. You are beginning to grow up. One day soon you will be as beautiful as I am—'

Even in the dream Jess giggled. 'You are *vain*, Cat!'

'Nonsense. I am absolutely gorgeous. And you will be too, mark by words. And one day you will have children of your own, and then it will be their world, too. You must look after it. You must try to do good to make your world a happier place. You won't need magic – just be your own dear self.'

Jess smiled in the dream and felt a great flood of warmth and happiness within her. Cat faded, and drifted away, leaving a faint hint of perfume behind and the feel of her hands on Jess's face. The bed became deeper, a snug, safe hollow that Jess sank into, heavy and drugged with sleep, happy and contented. She sank down into the magic of the dream itself and drowsily watched the glowing world slowly turning, turning, wheeling around on its age-old journey among the sharp, sleepless, crystal stars . . .

In the morning, Jess awoke still half in the dream. She was not sure that she felt real. She drifted down the stairs and was unsurprised to find Cat's things in the hall just inside the front door – her muddle of old cardboard boxes, carrier bags and bundles of new clothes carelessly tied up with string.

'So you *are* going, then?' she said to Cat, who

appeared at that moment from the kitchen. 'I sort of dreamed that you were.'

'Yes. My job is done. You are quite safe now, my little periwinkle. You have Toni and Gary to look after you, and Ginger to be your friend and especially Hyacinth to love you. I shall leave Clara to take care of the money.'

Jess bit her lip. 'Do you *have* to go?'

'You know I do. There are others like you, out there in the world, that need doing good to . . . It is what I am for.' Cat smiled, almost wistfully, almost sadly. 'There is such a lot for me to do. I expect you can imagine.'

'Will you ever come back?'

'If you really needed me, I would. I would know. But you won't. Everything is all right, and you will be too busy and too happy to need me.'

She looked at Jess fondly for a long moment. 'Better call the others to say goodbye,' she said gently.

They all stood on the steps in the morning sunshine while Gary loaded Cat's things into Mini. Flora watched with big eyes, one arm wrapped firmly around Hyacinth's left leg, as Cat shook hands with Toni and then kissed him on both cheeks in the Italian fashion. 'Feed them well, Toni,' she commanded. 'Jess is still a bit too thin.'

'*I'm* not,' said Toby.

'Well, of course, frogs *should* be well padded,' said Cat seriously. 'I'm sure you'll make some princess very happy.' Toby shut up.

She hugged Hyacinth hard, while Gary stuffed the last of the boxes somehow into Mini. 'You will love them, won't you?' she said. 'Whatever they do?'

Hyacinth wiped her eyes. 'You just leave that to

me,' she said firmly. 'Lovin' is one thing I'm good at and I don't need tellin' *how*!'

Gary grinned widely. 'None better,' he said. 'Don't you worry, Cat – the kids won't come to any harm, not with my girl in charge.'

'And you, too,' smiled Cat. 'You are a tower of strength, you are. I know a good man when I see one—' she winked at Hyacinth '—and *I* don't need telling how!'

She went to shake him by the hand, but Gary was not having any of that. He grabbed her in a huge bear-hug and gave her a great big smacking kiss.

'Gosh!' said Cat. 'That was nice. Got any more?'

'Stop it, you two!' ordered Hyacinth, wagging a finger. 'Gary – behave yourself!'

Cat took Ginger by the hand. 'You don't need any magic, Ginge – you make your own. Stick by them all, promise? They need you. And look after Mr Menon for me – *such* a nice man; so clever.' Poor Ginge didn't seem able to speak.

'Flora-dora – feed the ducks, hey?' She swung Flora up into the air, tickled her tummy and made her squeal. 'Go and see the Little Green Man after I've gone – I *think* he can turn cartwheels now.'

'Toby!' She ruffled his uncombed hair. 'Now *do* remember to examine your toes *every* day without fail.'

'Why?'

'In case the webs start growing, of course. Gronk-gronk, rivet-rivet! Seriously, nip down to the Do-It-Yourself shop at the end of the High Street in a minute. They're chucking out some packing-cases made of the most marvellous soft wood, super for making models and so on. Too good to miss.'

'Great!' said Toby, and grinned at Ginger, who gave the thumbs-up sign.

Last of all, Cat stood in front of Jess, placed her hands on the thin shoulders and looked gravely into her eyes. Jess didn't cry. Not quite. Cat said nothing for what seemed like a long time. Then she leaned forward, kissed Jess softly on the cheek, and whispered, 'It's your world.'

That was all.

Then she turned briskly to the others. 'Be good, all of you, won't you! Well – sort of good.' She frowned, looking slightly confused. 'I'm not sure I quite mean that . . . Let me put it this way – *don't do anything I wouldn't do!*'

They all roared with laughter – especially Gary – and even Jess had to join in. Cat grinned wickedly, waved, and slid into Mini's driving seat. The little car started at once with a cheerful roar and a boisterous cloud of blue smoke. A long, elegant arm waved from the driver's window, Mini seemed to leap sideways into the traffic—

—and she was gone.